When last we joined our story's protagonists . . .
D'oh!
An other-dimensional villain named Rȩżżőch was up to no good . . .
WHAT OF THE KEY? WHAT KEY WILL BE USED TO OPEN THE TREE OF ENTRY AND BRING ME INTO THE WORLD?
OOH! MY NAME IS THRULL AND I GOT THIS.
A betrayal most heinous, indeed.

Rężżöch and Thrull were vanquished with the aid of new allies. . . .
And I would have gotten away with it too, if it wasn't for you meddling kids.
Evil was sent back whence it came.
Our heroes dined on a mighty feast.
Whew! I'm sure there will be no new problems from here on out, right, guys?
. . . Guys?
Jack could not have been more wrong. Because . . .

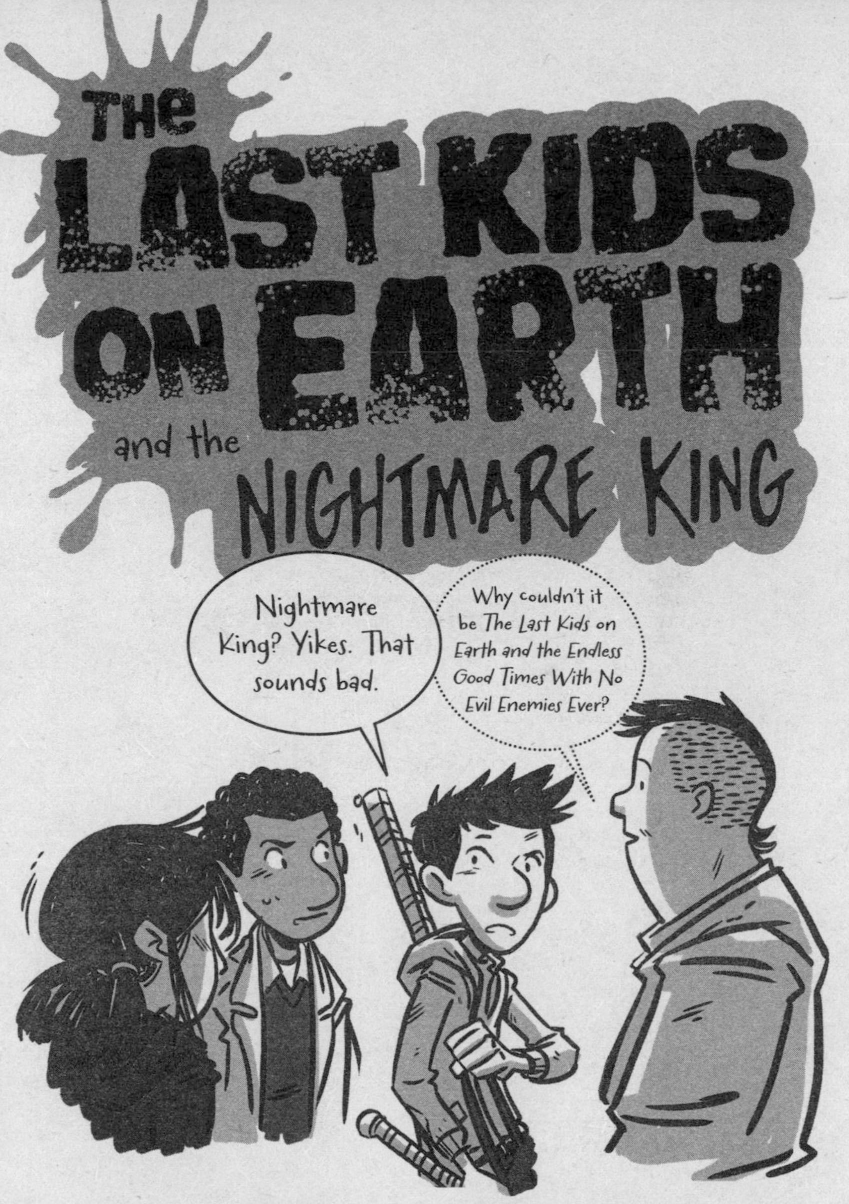

MAX BRALLIER & DOUGLAS HOLGATE

SCHOLASTIC INC.

ISBN 978-1-338-21663-9

Published by Scholastic Inc., 557 Broadway, New York, NY 10012, by arrangement with Viking Children's Books, an imprint of Penguin Young Readers Group, a division of Penguin Random House LLC.

12 11 10 9 8 19 20 21 22 23

Printed in the U.S.A. 40

First Scholastic paperback printing, September 2018

Book design by Jim Hoover
Set in Cosmiqua Com and Carrotflower

For Chewy—always and forever
ready for adventure. Catch you
on the flip-flop, good buddy.

—M. B.

For Scott, Ainslie, and Reuben

—D. H.

Map of Wakefield
Home Depot
Town forest
Fire station
Real-Life Super Mario Kart course
CVS
Town park (now thick with Vine-Thingies)
Quint's house
The Old Box Factory (known Dozer lair)
The docks (sea monsters!?)
Parker Middle School

Old Marsh Swamp
Atlantic Supermarket
Train tracks (home of the Tentacle Demon)
Town Square (home of our tree house, Joe's Pizza, and good-dude monsters!)
Old south graveyard
Big Al's Junk Palace (zombie cluster)
Burger King
Circle One Mall (home of the Wormungulous)

Chapter One

Want to know what the most fantastically radical game *ever* is?

I can tell you.

It's Real-Life *Super Mario Kart*.

And we're playing it right now.

My best buddies—Quint, June, and Dirk—are racing through town in post-apocalyptic vehicles of awesomeness: souped-up bumper cars that we call BoomKarts.

Dirk built the BoomKarts, and Quint loaded 'em up with wicked vehicular combat coolness: paintball blasters, defensive marble spillers, spiked tires, gas-powered slingshots—the works.

But me, Jack Sullivan? I don't need a BoomKart because I race atop my awesome monster-dog, Rover.

There's a reason for this game of Real-Life *Super Mario Kart*. I noticed that the energy and enthusiasm levels of my buddies were a little low. I mean, I was having trouble distinguishing them from the zombies. . . .

So I was like, "WE NEED EXCITEMENT! And what's more exciting than building an epic go-kart course with jumps, oil slicks, and a spinning speedway through creepy old man Aiken's house?"

That's one of the perks of life after the Monster Apocalypse—you can build giant Mario Kart–style tracks through your hometown.

Right now, June's winning, and I *must* take her out! She's claimed first place *three races in a row*! I yank my T-shirt cannon from Rover's saddlebag and . . .

Free T-shirt for ya, June!
SHIRT SLUG!

Direct hit! June's kart slices around the corner, spins, then *slams* into the local fire station.

"Don't mess with the king!" I shout. Rover woofs triumphantly as we stampede into first place. But I throw a glance behind me and see June's BoomKart is all busted up.

Crud. The idea is to win, not to knock your buddies unconscious! I know a good amount about buddies, 'cause I have the *best* buddies, and I'm quite sure they don't like being knocked out.

I tug on Rover's reins and he turns. "June, you okay?" I begin to call out, but then—

Yeah, I'm okay.
Okay with BENDING THE RULES TO BLAST YOU!
SURPRISE FOOTBALL CROSSBOW BOOM!

THWACK! The football knocks me clean out of Rover's saddle. I fall onto the grass. Surprise football crossbow booms are *the worst*.

"Your problem, Jack, is that you're too *nice*," June teases. "You don't have that competitive spirit like me."

She's about to speed ahead when something INSANE happens.

And I don't use the term "INSANE" lightly, since pretty much everything that happens during the Monster Apocalypse could be classified as insane or, at the very minimum, pretty much bonkers bananas.

We hear a voice.

A *human* voice.

I can't make out the words, but the voice is coming from inside the fire station. We've seen or heard *zero other humans* since the Monster Apocalypse began. So like I said, yeah, INSANE.

June and I are instantly hurrying to the station and pressing our ears to the red metal door.

We hear the voice again.

June looks at me, eyes bulging. CONFIRMED: this is both INSANE *and* BONKERS BANANAS.

I spin around, cupping my hands to my mouth. "Quint! Dirk! Time-out!"

“No way, friend!” Quint shouts as his BoomKart whips around the corner. “Not falling for that ruse again!”

“Not a ruse time-out! A real time-out!” I shout. “Really real!”

June points out that I should *not* be yelling, since we have *no clue* who is inside the fire station. Good point. I do a quick brain scan of possibilities—and the results are pretty gnarly. . . .

Terrifying Wasteland Marauders!

POSSIBLY INSIDE AT THIS VERY MOMENT!

Tires screech, and Quint and Dirk skid to a stop and hop from their BoomKarts. “What’s up?” Dirk asks.

“Human-sounding voices,” June whispers. “Inside the fire station!”

“We’ve never investigated the fire station,” Quint says. “I am quite curious.”

“Of course you’re curious!” I say. “We haven’t heard a single other human voice in months! We’ve heard *monster* voices, but those are all, like, *deep* and monster-y. The only human voices we’ve heard are *our own*.”

Suddenly, my mind is in a whole different place, thinking about how I had no idea my voice was nasally, and could that possibly explain years of difficulty making friends, 'cause who wants to be friends with the kid with the lousy voice, but if it's nasally, why did no one tell me before, I could have worked on it, even tried to put on a cool Australian accent or something, maybe even—

"Jack!" June snaps me back to attention, hooking a thumb at the fire station door. Dirk is tugging the handle, opening the door, and—

FIREFIGHTER ZOMBIES!
UHHHGGHNNN!

"Watch out!" June cries. A hefty undead fire chief is swiping at Quint!

Quint immediately curls up into a ball and plays dead like it's a bear attack. Thankfully, Dirk is there. He snags both zombies by their ankles and using his ludicrous strength—

We hurry inside the station before the other zombies can get their awful arms around us. Rover bolts in behind us, barely squeezing through, and—*SLAM!*—I throw the door shut.

The fire station is chilly, and the whole place smells like rotted people and spoiled cheesesteaks and old Chinese takeout.

But what, exactly, do we see inside?

Pretty much nothing. Now that the zombies are gone, the fire station is empty.

So *who* did we just hear talking? It definitely wasn't the zombies, 'cause they don't talk—they moan.

"C'mon," I say. "We'll check every room. *Someone* was in here yapping away."

Moving together for prime safety and battle readiness, we search the station.

We soon determine that there is no one else—zombie or non-zombie—inside the station. I lean against a dusty fire truck. "I don't get this," I say. "We heard voices!"

And then it happens. Again.

IT.

Capital letters "IT" 'cause IT is BIG.

We hear the voice. It's coming from a radio. . . .

My heart just about seizes up and my blood starts pumping to the rhythm of *Holy. Moley. Holy. Moley. Holy. Moley.*

June dashes toward the radio, kneeling, practically sliding across the floor. "We're here!" she cries. "We are here! Come in! Repeat, we are here! Other people! Humans! Four of us!"

And then it comes again: "REPEATING, THIS IS—*STATIC, CRACKLE*—WE ARE—*CRACKLE*—RESPOND IF—*STATIC*—WE WILL TRY AGAIN IN—*STATIC, CRACKLE*—"

The radio cuts off completely then. No hissing static. Just total silence. The broadcast, it appears, is over.

June gently reaches out and places her hand on the radio, like it's some ancient magic artifact. Her eyes are saucers. "I don't get it. I tried to respond," she says. "But they didn't hear. . . ."

After a quick examination of the radio, Quint says, "We *can't* respond. This is a radio *scanner*—one way only."

June sinks. "Oh."

"Do not distress," Quint says. "Simply *hearing* from other humans is huge! However, the signal is weak. That's why there was so much static. Let's get it back to the tree house. I can look into amplifying the signal."

June looks hard at the radio. She gently chews her lower lip, and then she just about explodes . . .

Humans! We heard other humans!
Indeed! We will take the radio with us. With any luck, they will try again.

Dirk just stands stiff, arms crossed. But after a moment, his mouth forms a wide, square smile.

My friends are just *really really happy*. And there isn't much that's better than watching your friends be just *really really happy*.

I once heard some old gray-haired lady say that the best part of holidays was *giving* gifts, not getting them. And I thought, lady, you're a lunatic—

getting a bunch of stuff is the total greatest. Now I grew up an orphan, so holidays were never, like, *Home Alone*–style *big*, but still, c'mon. Free gifts, yo!

But now I understand what that old gray-haired lady meant.

"Well, come on! Let's go!" June exclaims. "What are we waiting for?! Whoever's talking—we've got to find them! Now! No delay!"

Quint shakes his head. "June, we don't know where to start. When the Monster Apocalypse began, there were rumors that some people had gone out west. But that was months ago! That broadcast could be coming from *anywhere*! A different country, even! We need to know *where* those humans are before we do anything."

"Oh," June says. "Right."

Suddenly, I have this odd feeling in my stomach—a creeping feeling of confused fright.

"Guys," I say. "I just want to point out—the voice was really static-y and faint."

June squeezes my hand. "Jack, that doesn't matter. What matters is, there are people still alive. There are other humans out there! We are *not* the last—"

KA-KRAK!

The fire station shakes, shudders, and bits of tile and dust sprinkle down. Something just *landed* on the roof. . . . Something big.

Dirk and I head to the third floor to check out the roof situation. I quietly hoist open a window—whatever is on the roof is *big*, and I have zero interest in alerting it to my presence.

"Be careful," Dirk says.

"Look who you're talking to!" I reply, grinning as I bump his fist.

"I know who I'm talking to. That's why I said it."

"Yeah, yeah," I mutter. I inch out the window and onto the ledge. I shimmy over and grip the drainpipe.

Glancing down, I notice that the firefighter zombies are gone. Whatever this big thing on the roof is *scared* the zombies away. And I don't like that. . . .

Pulling my way up, I peek over the ledge.

And I gulp.

A big gulp.

Not a Big Gulp like a 7-Eleven soda. A big gulp like I just swallowed a softball.

SKRUNCH . . .

I'm looking at some sort of terrible flying beast. This monster slightly resembles a Winged Wretch, but it's, like—WAY BIGGER and WAY MORE BLOODCURDLING. Oh, and if you're unfamiliar, this is a Winged Wretch. . . .

Remember these evil goons?

I haven't made a sound, but the monster's head suddenly swings down toward me. As if he *senses* me there. His eyes, like, *look* into mine and it's totally freaky and I feel frozen. This thing is horribly horrifying. There are scars on his face, like he's been around the block a few times. Fear causes my fingers to squeeze the drainpipe, gripping tighter and tighter and, well . . .

A moment later, Dirk is yanking the entire drainpipe inside. I scramble off, happy to be on solid ground. I rush downstairs and my voice cracks as I say: "Dudes. It's bad. The thing up there is like a Winged Wretch but *bigger*!

REALLY BIG. And not pleasant looking. I know everyone's excited about the radio, but we are now trapped *inside* this fire station."

"I must remind you," Quint says, "it is very important that we escape with both our lives *and* the radio."

"We could just wait the monster out?" June suggests.

The instant June says that, the building quakes and ceiling chunks crash to the floor. The monster's talons are tightening around the walls.

"I don't think waiting him out is an option. . . ." I say quietly.

So with that, I announce a plan that kind of sounds thought-out, but I'm actually totally making up as I go. "Here's the deal," I say. "I'm going to ride Rover *straight* out, a full-on stampede. That will distract this big flying freak while you hop in your BoomKarts and escape. Then we'll meet back at the tree house. Fun, right? Smart, right? Brave, right?"

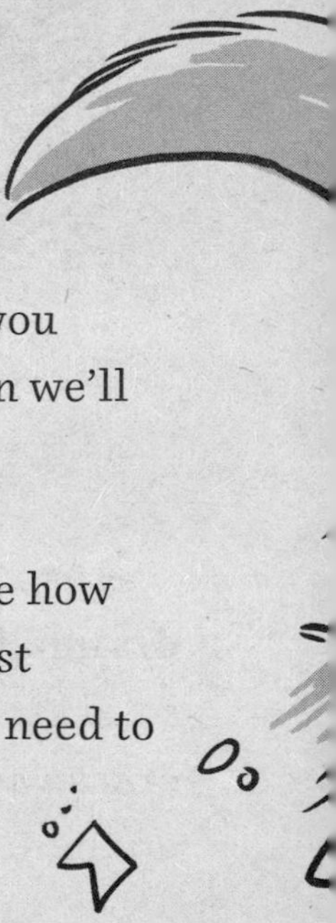

Everyone begins protesting, telling me how dumb that plan is, but in my head I'm just thinking that right now, this moment—I need to protect my buddies.

I take the radio from June—and I can see she's reluctant to let it go. "Don't worry," I say as I slip the radio into Rover's saddlebag. "I'll keep it safe. Promise."

And before anyone can say anything else, Dirk's lifting the fire engine garage door open, and . . .

Chapter Two

I hear a swirling, deafening thunderclap, followed by the sound of walloping wings and crumbling brick. I throw a glance over my shoulder. The flying terror is rocketing after us.

"This may not have been an A-plus plan, Rover. Possibly more of a C-minus plan. So . . . *FASTER!*" I cry, and Rover's paws slam the pavement.

The monster's wings are beating, air clapping, the sound of the swooping louder and louder. I feel the airborne enemy at my back, and then—

I smack into the street, flipping and flopping like a fish. My nose cracks against my knee, and I immediately feel blood bubbling inside my nostrils. I ignore it, suck air, then scramble to my feet—just in time to see the beast's massive front talons pierce Rover's hide.

Rover yelps as—

"NO!" I shriek.

The monster zooms low, dragging Rover across the pavement. The sound of pained scraping fills my ears while dread floods my stomach.

Rover suddenly snarls and—*SLASH!*—strikes with his claws, smacking the Wretch's talons. Rover is released. He *plunges* into the pavement—cracking, bouncing, and flipping across the ground.

He rolls to a stop.

He's on his side.

Not moving.

"Rover!" I cry as I speed down the street. My monster-dog has been hauled and tossed, like, fifty feet. "Oh no," I say, dropping to one knee beside him.

I scratch the thick, soft hair behind Rover's ears.

We'll get you fixed up. Don't worry. But we need to get you out of here. Now.

The monster's wings beat and snap. He's swooping toward me and Rover, returning to finish what he started.

But then I hear voices yelling.

I snap my head around and see my friends—

Quint is a very literal person.

But the beast is not distracted.

The monster's focus is only on Rover and me. He screams through the sky. His wings smack the ground, and debris whirls as he rockets toward us.

Three hundred feet and closing in.

Two hundred feet and closing in.

One hundred feet and closing in.

The monster's dragon-like mouth opens, and I see an army of thick fangs. I gulp. But suddenly, the monster's wings snap to his sides and his legs stab forward.

KA-KRAK!

It feels like an earthquake as his talons *slam* into the street, claws digging into the asphalt.

I crane my neck to look up at the monster—and I see him, fully and 100 percent clearly for the first time. He is bigger than any Winged Wretch. In fact, it's more like . . .

Battle scars.

Bone wings.

The King Wretch!
Ginormous jaws.
Freaky-deaky swirly eyeballs.
Bloodcurdling action pose.
Razor-sharp talons.

The smell of my own blood in my nose does nothing to lessen the terror. But Rover yowls behind me, and my fear is replaced by *furious rage* at the big ugly fiend that hurt my friend.

I draw my blade—the Louisville Slicer. It's basically my post-apocalyptic baseball bat version of a lightsaber.

It is the weapon that felled Blarg, the ancient evil.

It is the weapon that sliced open the great Wormungulous.

It is the weapon that, hopefully, is going to save our butts right now.

I step forward, putting myself between the King Wretch and my injured friend. The monster takes heavy, planet-rocking steps forward until he towers over Rover and me.

My mouth is dry. It takes me a moment to speak—but when I do, I roar—

BACK OFF!
Rover is my friend, and I don't let jerk monsters steal my friends!

The King Wretch's colossal cranium dips and lowers until we're nearly eye to eye. The monster glances down at Rover and then up to me—staring into my eyes, peering into my pupils.

Something catches in my throat. The back of my neck goes tingly.

And then I feel soda bubbles in my brain. . . .

Chapter Three

It's like the King Wretch looks *through* my eyeballs, beyond, and straight into my brain—like he's gazing deep into my soul. My vision clouds. Everything begins to go black.

My body is loose. Wobbly.

It's strange, but—I think I'm falling asleep. On my feet. Everything is becoming very—

SCREECH!

Squealing tires snap me out of my strange waking slumber. I manage to turn and see—

The King Wretch glances at my friends and our BoomKart weaponry, then his head swings back to me. There's something in his chilling eyes and dripping fangs that resembles a sly smile. I see—*I know*—this monster has *zero* fear of me or my buds.

But he leaves anyway.

The King Wretch gives me a final look—a once-over—and then shoots into the sky with a burst of beating wings. His tail snaps the pavement as he rockets away, winging, curving, and slicing into the distance.

The soda bubbles in my brain are fading away and my head is feeling halfway normal again. I drop to my buddy. "Rover, you okay?"

Rover shakes his head like he's knocking the cobwebs loose, then gets to his feet. He looks okay, although there's an *anger* on his face that I've never seen—like he wouldn't mind seeing that King Wretch again.

Like he wouldn't mind a bit of revenge.

Suddenly, June gasps. She's frantically ripping open Rover's saddlebag. "The radio!" she exclaims. "It's busted up!"

June's face has gone pale and she looks like she's about to vomit, but Quint and Dirk save the moment.

"I promise to repair it, June," Quint says.

"Like the geek said," Dirk adds, "we'll fix it. No question."

June nods and breathes a shaky sigh of relief. "Okay . . ."

I stare into the distance. I watch the King Wretch fading, getting small, and finally disappearing behind the crumbling Wakefield skyline.

With any luck, that's the last we'll be seeing of that beast.

Dudes, I think that's enough adventuring, and enough almost dying, for one day.
Let's get back to the Town Square, huh?

So things are different now.

A lot different.

And not just different since before the Monster Apocalypse.

I mean different since the last time you saw us. In the past month, things have changed A TON.

Here's a quick recap for those, like myself, with crummy memories. Six months ago, there was a Monster Apocalypse. Doors opened above the Earth, and suddenly monsters and beings from a different dimension were propelled into our world—along with the horrible zombie plague. It looked a bit like this. . . .

A bunch of these monsters took up residence at our local slice shop, Joe's Pizza. And they weren't evil—they were terrifying-at-first-but-totally-friendly-in-the-end monsters.

However, *one* of the monsters was actually pure evil. His name was Thrull, and he worshipped the diabolical ultra-villain Ŗeżżőcħ the Ancient, Destructor of Worlds. Thrull was trying to bring Ŗeżżőcħ to Earth so that

Ŗeżżőcħ *could devour and destroy our planet*.

Me, my human buddies, and the Joe's Pizza monster crew teamed up to defeat Thrull and Ŗeżżőcħ. But Ŗeżżőcħ *may* try to return. See, he's got a whole Emperor Palpatine vibe to him. Very sinister, possibly bad skin.

So these days, my human buddies and the good-dude monsters live in awesome harmony in Wakefield Town Square. It used to be a boring old suburban town. But now it's Monster City!

When my friends and I get back from our run-in with the King Wretch, we're greeted by Biggun. He's the biggest of all the friendly monsters. He stands guard at the entrance to the Town Square, day and night, rain or shine or regular in-the-middle cloudiness. Doesn't talk. He's basically the town bouncer.

The monsters have turned the crumbling Wakefield Town Square into a busy, bustling monster home—a place where all are welcome.

"Hey-ya, Jack!" a monster named Pogvane says.

"Dirk, we arm wrestling later?" the monster Etagg calls out.

"June, you must show me how to prepare your fried macaroni recipe!" another monster says.

Strolling through town, my heart swells. I've just never felt more complete. It's like walking down the hall at school, and everyone knows you, everyone says hey, everyone wants to chat. It's a feeling I'd never had—a feeling I could only imagine until now.

It's *camaraderie*.

Besides that awesome human-monster camaraderie, the best part of our Town Square home is that it's *totally* zombie-free—and that's thanks to our monster friend Bardle. . . .

-Bardle-
General sort of wizardly vibe.
Radical swords for when it's time to get stabby.
Total grump face—but he's actually very sweet when you get to know him.

Bardle and Quint designed torches to keep the zombies away. You know those candles you light in the summer to keep mosquitos away? It's like that. We call them Zom-B-Gone torches. They surround the Town Square, so we don't have to worry about zombies popping up at inopportune moments and, y'know, *eating us*.

The Zom-B-Gone torches might maybe work on Winged Wretches, too, because other than that big ol' King Wretch, we haven't seen many of those around lately. Not that I'm complaining.

Anyway, in Wakefield Town Square, there's *always* something fun going down. For example:

- One day, it's the monster Muldrurd having a sale on newly crafted arms and armor. Another day, it's a rock-eating contest.

- There's a weekly wrestling match where these two big lugs—Thonn and Gronn—duke it out. They got the idea after I showed them an old episode of *WWE Raw* I had on DVD.

- Sometimes at night, we watch movies. Y'know, to show the monsters about life on Earth—and to show them that movies are the best.

There are restaurants, too. The monsters are still learning how to cook with Earth food—a few of their things came through the portal with them, but not much. The food is—well—*interesting*. . . .

After we grab a bite, Quint yawns. "I'm exhausted from the day's adventures. And I should get to work on repairing the radio."

"Yes!" June exclaims. "No dillydallying. Straight to work, Quint."

I won't lie—I'm beat, too. And a little freaked from the King Wretch encounter. So we head home. Home is a tree house—and the tree house is mind-clobberingly *cool*. . . .

Thrull damage.
Helidrone launch pad.
Bottle-rocket launchers.
Thrull damage.
Blast-the-Dirk cannon.
Crossbow.
Rainwater shower.
Weatherproof flat-screen TV.
Electric generator and BoomKart charging station.
Armory, gadget storage, and Bestiary lockbox.
Outer defenses (sharp!).

The tree house *used* to be in my backyard. But—thanks to a monster called the Wormungulous—the whole thing was transplanted here, downtown, into the Joe's Pizza parking lot. . . .

So this is life right now.

And as we stroll back to the tree house, I'm thinking that life is good!

In fact, life is *perfect*!

Of course, in a post-Monster-Apocalypse world, life is never perfect for long. . . .

Chapter Four

Just a few days later, I'm up early, playing with my Helidrone. I hang beef jerky off it, and Rover tries to pluck it in midair.

That's when Quint calls me up to the tree house. Minutes later, we're all gathered upstairs—me leaning against the doorway, trying to look Star-Lord cool.

Quint has a smile on his face that's different from any Quint smile I've seen before. Closest comparison: when we got opening night, midnight tickets to see the second Avengers movie.

The look is a mixture of shock and excitement—like he won the dork lottery.

He flicks on the radio, and the little light turns green. It's working!

"I repaired it. But the issue," Quint says, "is the range of the antenna. I need parts to make the antenna fully functional. But I *can* and *will*. Soon, we will be able to listen to whoever is talking out there."

June looks at Quint, down at the radio, and then back to Quint. And she erupts. . . .

Quint, you magnificent basket case! That's fantastic!

Quint is beaming. I see tears in June's eyes. Big, fat, happy tears. "Jack, isn't this wonderful?"

"Um, *yes*!" I say. "Imagine the cool stuff we can do now! We can meet monsters! We can trade weapon designs! Exchange key information about Ŗeżżőcħ! We need to learn radio jargon—I want to know *all* that classic long-haul truck driver lingo."

And suddenly, I'm imagining myself as a tough guy post-apocalyptic truck driver—possibly the most macho job ever. . . .

Breaker, breaker—situation dire. Low on gas. Butt cheeks asleep. Monsters on the horizon.

"Jack," June says, snapping me out of my end-of-the-world truck driver fantasies. "Jack, my *parents*. Our *families*. We can find out where they are. Remember what I told you, at the school?"

I think back to that moment on our middle-school roof, many months ago. . . .

My parents are out there, Jack.
I saw them. And someday we're gonna be reunited!

"Of course! That too!" I say. "I mean—that's fantastic. Right? Obviously fantastic. Finding your parents. Good. Great."

I look to Quint. He still has that odd smile on his face. "Quint, buddy. Who knows . . . You might get to see your family again."

Quint exhales very slowly, then nods. The corner of his mouth is upturned in a cautious smile.

And again I feel that anxious, sweaty, pit-in-the-stomach feeling I had at the fire station, when we first discovered it was a radio making the noise.

My head starts spinning. Dirk and June are discussing the radio, and Quint is already sketching plans for how to boost the range. My friends' voices swirl around me, and I feel sweat pouring down my forehead. I try to swallow, but my mouth is desert dry.

"Guys, I just need a little fresh, um, what's the word . . . Fresh cookies . . . ? Fresh breath? I mean . . . ah . . . fresh air, I think. . . ." My voice trails off as I step through the door, out onto the deck. It's late autumn—or as I call it, "fancy fall"—and the air is cool.

But my entire body is hot.

My heart is palpitating. I have a palpitating heart. And that's a BAD KIND OF HEART!

Why? What's happening?

Like—like, *panic*. Real panic. I'm *freaking out*. And I don't know why!

My legs feel wobbly and useless. I need a cool

drink. I'd kill for an ice-cold Capri Sun. I reach into our rainwater collector, scoop some water into my hands, and splash it on my face.

"JACK!" a monstrous voice suddenly bellows

I blink. Looking down, I see the monster Skaelka in the Town Square. Her shouting pulls me out of my panic. Skaelka was a vicious warrior in the monster dimension: scary savage and fiercely ferocious, from the stories we've heard.

MY EAR NODULES DETECT SCREAMING FROM INSIDE YOUR TREE FORTRESS. ARE THERE VILLAINS PRESENT? DO YOU NEED MY AX?

"Huh?" I ask, my head still fuzzy. "Oh. No, no. We were just, um, celebrating. A few days ago, we—ah—we heard voices."

Skaelka's spinal-spikes flex—her sign of suspicion. "Voices! Inside your brain folds? Are you going insane? Should I put you down now by slicing off your head? I would be honored to perform the dance of decapitation on you, Jack."

"No. No, no," I say. "No decapitation dancing desired. Thanks, though. I meant, we heard voices on a radio."

"Radio?" Skaelka asks.

"Um. It's like a TV, but for sounds."

Skaelka thinks this over for a moment. "Fine. Inform me if you require decapitation services. Or if you discover you are going insane," she says, and she clomps away, dragging her massive ax. I think, *man*, I'm *really* glad that barbaric looney-tune is on our side.

I take three deep breaths, then I step back into the tree house. My friends are already celebrating. June is cranking up the speakers on her "bomb sound system" while Dirk shakes Sprite bottles and blasts soda around the tree house like we just won the World Series.

This radio changes *everything*.

Everyone joyous.

Everyone happy.

Everyone except for me.

And I think I know why.

If they get that radio really running—it won't be long before they get in touch with other humans. And maybe even their families.

And what happens to me then?

I have no parents to go home to. I have no one waiting for me. Everything I have: it's here.

I like our life *here*.

So I have only one choice.

I need to snatch that radio and SMASH IT AND DESTROY IT AND PREVENT MY FRIENDS FROM EVER LEAVING!

No, no.

Kidding. (Mostly.)

I need to show my friends that life here is so exceptionally, undeniably, crowd-pleasingly *perfect* that they'll never *want* to leave! If I can show my friends endless fun, maybe they'll just totally forget about the radio.

Maybe?

Hopefully?

There's only one way to find out. By becoming . . .

PROTECTOR OF FRIENDS, DEFENDER OF THE REALM, and MASTER, CREATOR, AND KEEPER OF ALL THINGS RADICALLY FUN!
SO COOL
CRACK

Chapter Five

Okay, so . . . my plan is not off to a good start. It's hard to make your friends want to stick around when stuff like this keep happening:

When I saw Quint about to get gobbled, I was like, "Oh crud! Stuff like that's only going to make Quint want to find his parents *more*! And that means he'll work *harder* to complete the radio! I must *immediately* put a stop to all potential Quint-eating incidents, and I must show Quint and the monsters a whole *mother lode of awesome*!"

This is my first chance to prove that I am master, creator, and keeper of all things radically fun. I'm checking the date on our calendar when I come up with a plan.

BTW: I'm obsessed with our calendar. I call it the Bubble Wrap Zombies of Wakefield Date Keeper. A big sheet of bubble wrap represents each month. When the day ends, we tack a photo of a zombie onto the date and pop the bubble. I am, naturally, Chief Zombie Photographer.

Anyway, I see it's been exactly *one month* since the monsters and us humans teamed up to defeat Thrull and stop Ŗeżżőcħ from devouring Earth. And that's the *perfect* excuse for a massive celebration—monsters and humans having a blast *together*!

First, I tell my human buds. "Guys!" I say. "What do you think about a sort of humans-versus-monsters *Olympics*? Like, a big bash: games during the day, a big BBQ at night!"

Dirk shrugs. June and Quint shoot me dagger eyeballs that say, "NO WAY. MUST WORK ON RADIO. RADIO IMPORTANT. GAMES NOT IMPORTANT."

June explains they're building something called a "long-range signal-boosting antenna."

Sigh, groan, and crud—curse that stupid, good-for-nothing radio! Curse it to the seas, I say!

But I don't give up and I don't get down (except on the dance floor, where I *always* get down, 'cause I'm an absolute tornado of rhythmic ridiculousness).

Anyway, after a full day of me popping up and bugging my friends about the games nonstop . . .

June and Quint *finally* give in after I burst into the tree house and blast them with our supercharged leaf blower. Quint says to June, "A day of fun could do us some good. . . . We must let our brains rest sometimes."

June, who needs Quint's mega-brain well rested so he can complete the radio, relents as well. And Dirk just shrugs as usual and says, "A'ight."

"BOMB!!" I exclaim. "Yes, yes, yes!"

In a flash, I'm zip-lining from the tree house to Joe's Pizza—where I announce to the town . . .

Monster friends!
I hereby propose the first-ever Monsters versus Humans Almighty Ultra-Important Tournament Games.
WOOO!

Bardle is kind of the monsters' representative, so he and I sit down and decide on nine events. In the spirit of unity and community and junk, we pick a mix of human games and monster games. . . .

The Monsters vs. Humans Almighty Ultra-Important Tournament Games

- Kickball
- Dodgeball
- Tail-Wrestling
- Human Tossing
- Street Fighter
- Helidrone Flying
- Car Crushing
- Tug-of-War
- Projectile Fire Puking

Blakon, who's like a monster-carpenter, even designs a trophy for the winner. It's *awesome*—

The Ridonculous Radical Triumph Trophy

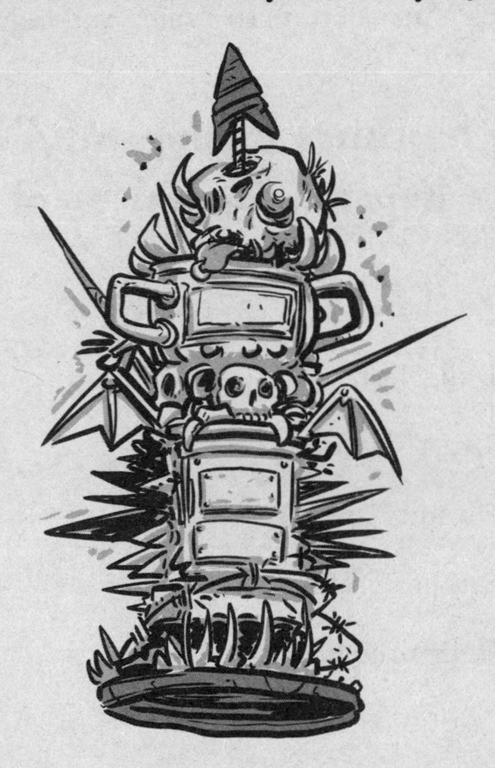

That night, we're all in the Town Square, gathered around the trophy.

"That trophy is rad," June says. "I'll admit, I was kinda anti-games—but now I for real seriously want to win."

"Then let's get our rest," I say. "The games

begin tomorrow morning. And if we want that trophy, we need to CRUSH IT."

We are not crushing it.

In fact, we're *being* crushed. We're being mashed, macerated, and mangled by these monsters.

The games kicked off at 8 a.m. sharp, and it was bad news from the beginning. Each event begins with me announcing (screaming, really) the name of the game. The day starts down by the used-car lot, with me shouting: "TOURNAMENT GAME: TUG-OF-WAR!"

Tug-of-War does not go well. . . .

We're now five events in—the monsters have won THREE and we've won TWO. Even when we lose, though, it's a total blast. Playing regular ol' games is just way better after the end of the world, 'cause you can play wherever you want!

At Indiana's Antiques, we enjoy the most expensive game of dodgeball in history. . . .

At Walmart, I scream: "TOURNAMENT GAME: KICKBALL!" and then we're booting the ball and speeding and sliding down the slippery Walmart aisles.

Us humans get a break there, because the monster Grehrall punctures the ball with one of his gnarly head horns, and Quint—who's a stickler for the rules, blows the whistle. . . .

We do even *worse* at the games the monsters choose.

Skaelka shouts, “TOURNAMENT GAME: HUMAN TOSSING,” and I’m immediately cursing myself for agreeing to that one. . . .

But there's *one* category of games we totally stomp the monsters at: games that require being "dexterous," as Quint describes it. Basically, any game where you need nimble fingers. For example: video games. We play Street Fighter on the giant scoreboard at the high-school football field, and I destroy Skaelka with a Hurricane Kick and Shoryuken combo.

After eight games, the score is all tied up: MONSTERS: 4 and HUMANS: 4. There's only one event left: the Helidrone flying contest.

Quint is ecstatic. "Our agile fingers will allow us to defeat them!"

We all gather on the roof of the Dairy Queen. Unfortunately for Team Humans, it turns out the monster Blycas is, like, naturally gifted at flying RC helicopters.

"Did she just do a double loop-the-loop?!" I ask as I watch Blycas fly the drone.

"Unbelievable . . ." June mutters.

"I think I'm kind of into her," Dirk whispers.

After bringing the Helidrone in for a perfect landing, Blycas hands the controller to Quint. Before Quint begins, June grabs him by the collar and says, "Quint, I *hate* losing. Don't mess this up!"

Quint suddenly looks nervous. "It's just a

game, June," he says. "In the grand scheme of things, it's really not all that import—"

June yanks Quint so close they're practically butterfly kissing. She growls like grizzled, old-age Harrison Ford. "I want that *trophy*."

Oh, no. This is bad. Quint is *not* clutch.

Quint chokes!

In school, the kids even straight-up called him *Quint the Choker*! And not 'cause he's, like, bad at chewing and swallowing his food or something —but because when the pressure is on, the kid folds like a beach chair!

And the Helidrone flying contest is no different.

About thirty seconds after taking off, the Helidrone is upside down, spinning and spiraling through the air, skipping over a row of houses, and then plummeting toward the ground.

"MY HELIDRONE!" I shriek.

I scramble down the side of the Dairy Queen, hit the street, and race off in search of my crashed 'copter. . . .

Chapter Six

I'm majorly annoyed with myself. I never should have let the Helidrone be used in the games. Rover loved chasing the thing, and I *hate* the thought of it lying busted somewhere.

I'm hiking down a hill, past a crumpled old

shed, when I spot the Helidrone. And I realize it may be lost forever. . . .

From where I'm standing, I see that it crash-landed inside Big Al's Junk Palace. Big Al's is a sprawling junkyard with twenty-foot walls covered in barbed wire. Hundreds of zombies surround the place. Undead moaning and the thick scent of decomposing skin float up toward me.

There'll be no retrieving my Helidrone—not right now, at least. . . .

I lift my head to the heavens and utter a short memorial for my flying friend. "You may be gone, Helidrone, but you are not forgotten. You were a first-class gizmo. A blue-ribbon gadget. You will be missed—but with any luck, you will not be missed for long. I *will* attempt to retrieve you, Helidrone."

I spit on the ground, then use my sneaker to rub the saliva into the dirt—because that seems like a kind of cool and theatrical thing to do after delivering a totally killer memorial speech.

I take the long way home. My path leads me through the eerie old playground outside the crumbling remains of the town preschool. It's super run-down and unsettling. Basically, it looked like a post-apocalyptic playground *before* the world went post-apocalyptic. Rusty swings blow gently in the wind, and paint-chipped seesaws jut out of the ground like prehistoric skeletons.

And then it gets a whole lot creepier. . . .

The stench of the beast hits me like a basketball to the face. You know the embarrassing face-hit you get in gym class when you're not paying attention and you just get straight *whammed* and you try to shrug it off like it's no biggie but secretly you're like, *oh-man-my-nose-the-pain-it-hurts-in-a-super-awful-way*. It's one of those.

And worst of all: I know this smell.

The tremendous beast Blarg stunk of it. The monstrous fiend Thrull reeked of it.

It is the odor of *evil*.

And the King Wretch oozes the foul odor. It seems to swirl off him. I didn't smell it at the fire station—probably because my nostrils were stuffed with blood.

The monster's head bobs, lowering, and his eyes narrow as he focuses on me.

I don't mean to, I don't *want* to, but I look into his eyes. Soda bubbles in my brain again. The King Wretch is, like, gazing into my insides.

I can't move.

I'm locked in. Inside my brain.

I feel something like a tornado of terrible energy whirl past me. *Through me*. I hear a very distant BOOM, and then everything is *altered*. . . .

I'm in a sort of *dream*. But this feels realer than any dream I've ever dreamed. It's like watching myself, like I'm on the outside, and I'm looking in.

And suddenly, I'm not at the playground anymore. I'm in Wakefield Town Square, and everything is different. The world is not back to normal, no, but it's better. The sky is bluer-than-blue and the sun is warm on my skin. Big, beautiful plants grow.

I feel *alive*. My entire body is buzzing, warm. I feel safe. I feel untouchable.

Invincible.

I come to the tree house. Looking up, I see that the tree is taller, thicker, and the tree house is now a tremendously huge sort of *tree castle*. Rooms and rooms on top of rooms, connected—a fortress fit for a king.

But who is the king?

I grip the ladder, and I climb.

My friends are inside.

Waiting for me.

June, Dirk, Quint, and Rover.

Rover leaps up onto me, but he doesn't knock me back—it's like I'm strong enough to hold him. Like we're equals.

My friends have huge, wide smiles on their faces, and their eyes glow with happiness.

And in the center, between them—a huge seat. A seat like . . . *a throne*.

I don't know how I know it, but I know this throne is for me.

So I sit.

Am I, like, a king?

I sit for what feels like a full hour, just enjoying the feeling of safety, of my friends close by.

And then I stand. In this strange dream-vision-thing, I step out onto the deck and see Wakefield, my town, sprawling out in front of me. There are no zombies.

My friends, the four of us, are safe. And there's a feeling in my stomach telling me that that safety will never go away.

The zombies are no threat.

Evil, giant monsters are no danger.

I *am* a king and I rule over something good, something secure, something vital. Something that will never be taken from me. Something that—

"Jack. JACK! JACK!"

It's Dirk.

But I look to Dirk in this strange dream, and he's not speaking. He's just standing beside my throne, smiling.

Then I hear it again. "JACK! JACK!"

And I realize Dirk is not screaming at me in this weird dream space. He's calling me for real.

Outside.

And suddenly—

"JACK!"

My mind comes screaming back to the present. I'm still in the spooky playground. I haven't moved an inch.

The King Wretch smiles, flashing vicious

fangs. And then he's stomping away, disappearing amongst the crumbling, ruined houses.

I hear my name called again. Turning, I see my friends trampling through the overgrown grass.

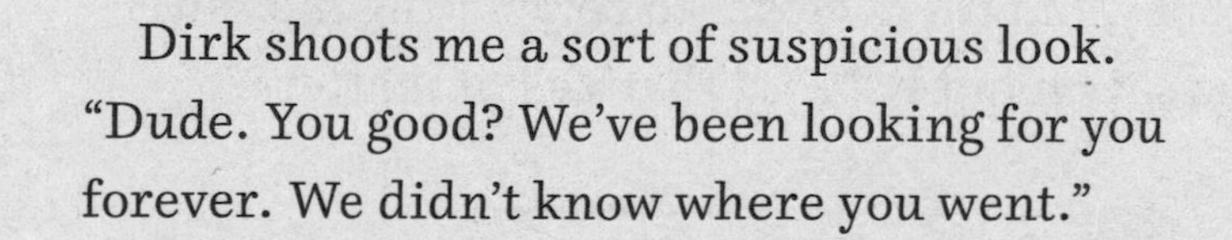

Dirk shoots me a sort of suspicious look. "Dude. You good? We've been looking for you forever. We didn't know where you went."

"I just went to find the Helidrone," I manage. I can still smell the faint odor of evil in the air—but no one else appears to notice it. The King Wretch disappeared before they arrived. I don't mention the monster—and I don't mention the strange dream-vision-thingy, either.

"Did you find it?" June asks.

"Um. Ah. Yes," I say after a long moment. "Yeah. It crashed in Big Al's Junk Palace. It's gonna be a real pain getting it back. . . ."

"Big Al's Junk Palace!" Quint exclaims. "OF COURSE! Instead of trying to build the radio antenna from scratch, we can simply find one there. I'm sure the junkyard will have what we need: *a long-range signal-boosting antenna*."

June lights up. "You think so?"

"Certainly!" Quint says.

One of the monsters shouts, "You lost the flying device?! That means . . . WE WIN! We have won!"

The monsters roar in celebration.

I look to June, worried she'll be upset about the loss—but she's beaming. "We may have lost the trophy, but we're closer to completing the radio," she says happily. "And that's what matters."

-Monster Bash!-

That night, we party *hard*.

First, there's a ceremony where the monsters receive the Ridonculous Radical Triumph Trophy. There's a big statue of some old town founder dude at the center of the town green, and the Ridonculous Radical Triumph Trophy is placed in his arms.

The monsters pose for a photo, and June and Dirk hurry in just as I snap the photo. . . .

Then there's a big BBQ with grilled Doritos, sizzling Sour Patch Kids, fresh fruit from Dirk's garden, and roasted SPAM burgers. We even have a karaoke dance-off. June crushes it, obviously.

The monsters are happy because they won, and my buddies are happy 'cause they're closer to having a fully functioning radio scanner. Everyone's having an absolute blast.

Everyone but me.

Because I am freaked: jittery-brained and atomically anxious. That King Wretch? He's more than just a regular old big monster. He's evil. I smelled it on him—the same evil stench that dripped from the villains Blarg and Thrull, the same evil stench that drips from Winged Wretches and Dozers. And the King Wretch isn't just evil—he's *evil with weirdo mystic powers*.

What sort of monster can put visions in my head? I've never seen or heard of anything like that before.

I should tell my friends.

But I'm doing everything I can to convince my buddies they're *safe* here! And if I tell them that the King Wretch is *hunting* me and giving me weird dream-vision-thingies—that'll just freak them out and give them even more reason to try to leave!

And also . . . the vision was *good*. I've seen a vision of the future (I know that sounds nuts, but the world is nuts now!), and that vision of the future was *okay*. We were safe! My monster buddies were safe! So there's nothing to be scared of.

Right?

I watch my friends: happy, enjoying the party—and for a moment, it seems to make sense. It's up to *me* to keep my buddies *here* and keep them *safe* and create that beautiful, kick-butt, zombie-free world the King Wretch showed me. I mean, I wouldn't have seen the vision if it wasn't the way the world was *supposed* to go!

I must keep them happy.

I must keep them enjoying this life.

Because that's what the vision told me to do. . . .

Chapter Seven

I'm itchy. Anxious. Straight-up squirrelly.

See, the first thing I learned after the Monster Apocalypse began is that you *need* to keep busy. Otherwise, you go crazy-pants. So . . .

I make a decision: I'm getting my Helidrone back from Big Al's Junk Palace.

I tell my buds, and they're *totally* on board with journeying to Big Al's, even if it's for different reasons. . . .

Big Al's Junk Palace will have the long-range signal-boosting antenna we need to complete the radio!
The radio is the key to getting in touch with the rest of humanity!
And I need a new lead pipe for monster bashing!

"Getting inside Big Al's will not be easy," Quint says. "We must perform reconnaissance from an elevated position to analyze all possible points of entry. A roof near Big Al's would be best."

I lean forward. "A roof, eh? Sounds to me like it's time for a game of . . . THE STREETS ARE LAVA!"

"Yes! Yes! Yes!" June screams.

"Capital idea, Jack!" Quint adds.

Okay, so . . . The Streets Are Lava is basically the best game ever. It's super simple, and you probably kinda know what the deal is. When you play at home, it's called The Floor Is Lava. You move around the house making tough leaps and grabs, while trying not to touch the ground. It's like, "Oh, Bill (or whatever your buddy's name is—if it's Bill, even better), jump from the coffee table to the couch, but *don't touch the floor!*" The game always ends with your mom's favorite vase shattering and everyone getting grounded for the weekend.

But see, *our* version is post-apocalyptic—so it's more adventurous and more dangerous, and *no one ever gets grounded!* The goal of the game is: GET AS FAR ACROSS OUR CRUMBLING TOWN AS POSSIBLE WITHOUT TOUCHING THE STREET.

It's crazy fun *and* we also discover all sorts of supplies and loot while playing. One game led us to a fancy-pants country club where we found an automatic tennis-ball-firing thing. We pushed the BallBlaster 2000 straight back home because, I mean—an automatic tennis-ball-firing thing? That's obviously fantastic fun.

I tighten my laces and get ready to head out.

"I'll grab my tools!" Dirk says.

"I'll grab my backpack!" June says.

"I'll pack a picnic lunch!" Quint says.

See what I mean? How could I let all this come to an end?

We start downtown, moving from one store rooftop to the next. Then we hit the houses, where it's roof to patio to tree. Then we're scaling a fire escape to the top of the 7-Eleven.

We've come to the 7-Eleven before, but we've never figured out how to get beyond it without breaking the rules of The Streets Are Lava. But now we *have to* figure it out so we can get to the Burger King that overlooks Big Al's. (And we have to stick to the rules. I will *not* disrespect the game by dismissing the rules all willy-nilly.)

Dirk slips off his backpack.

"Whatcha got there, Dirk?" I ask.

He grins. "Cowboy stuff. Like in the movies."

Dirk has *weird* taste in movies. Also, he gets on these kicks where he'll only watch one kind of movie, nonstop. First it was *only* WWE wrestling specials. Then it was *only* arm-wrestling movies—and there's only like two movies with arm-wrestling-centric plots, so that got old quick.

His latest kick is old Wild West Westerns. And I dig that, because my buddies and I *are* basically modern-day cowboys. We roam the land and battle wild enemies and don't shower very often.

Anyway, Dirk's fully obsessed with anything Wild West–y—including cowboy skills. . . .

The rope makes a *whift*, *whift*, *whift* sound as Dirk whirls then hurls the lasso. And he nails it, first try! "Told ya," he says, with a proud grin. "I'm *all* cowboy."

He spits on his hands, rubs his palms together, grins 'cause he knows that looks *cool*, and then grabs the rope and leaps. . . .

"Whoa!" June exclaims as we watch Dirk swing and then land expertly on the roof across the way. "That was, like, Olympic perfection!"

Dirk finds an old painter's ladder. We use it to bridge the gap between our rooftop and his, and then we non-cowboys hurry across.

The Burger King roof is huge and slanted, but

a bunch of cable and telephone wires run down the side of it, so we're able to climb our way up. And at the top, finally, we have a panoramic view of Big Al's Junk Palace.

We see it's going to be *really* hard to get inside. . . .

Stink odors.
General impenetrable-fortress vibe.

Now, *previously*, when we needed to get inside a place that was surrounded by zombies, we used *this* brilliant Quint invention—

—The Scream Machine—

The Scream Machine was a combo iPhone-loudspeaker-egg-timer. Set the timer and then the speaker would unleash a whole series of crazy-loud recordings of screams from movies.

Sadly, we lost our beloved Scream Machine a few weeks back when a horrifying monster straight up *ate* the thing. It was totally bone-chilling because the machine *kept on screaming* from inside the beast's stomach, and we could hear it emitting a chorus that sounded like a thousand frightened children. . . .

<BURP.>
RAWR. . . .
AIIIIEEEE!!!!

Without the Scream Machine, we need a new plan.

We plop down on the roof to think, and Quint gets out his picnic lunch.

Can I just say, real quick—picnics are the most *overrated thing ever*. I went on one picnic, one time, and it was lousy: my sandwich was soggy, there were red ants crawling in places where red ants shouldn't be crawling, and I got grass stains on my left butt cheek—and that's my favorite butt cheek! Why anyone would prefer a picnic lunch to a regular, normal, indoor lunch, I'll never know.

However, Quint's picnic lunch is much better than I expected *and* it's on a roof, so no grass on my butt and no red ants *anywhere*. Also, any regular activity done on a roof is automatically better. Playing Monopoly? Fun. Playing Monopoly on a roof? AWESOME.

Quint's "picnic basket" is in fact just a vintage *Transformers* lunchbox. And there's no variety of food inside—it's a box full of, like, nine thousand Reese's Pieces. So I guess the lesson here is: regular-world picnics are crummy; post-apocalyptic-action-plotting-rooftop-Reese's picnics are A-okay.

Quint proceeds to point out, in graphic detail, why each one of those ideas is "dangerously idiotic." And my buddy paints a vivid picture. . . .

“But do not fret!” Quint says, holding up a finger and looking maximally dorky. “I shall come up with a solution.”

June angrily hurls a fistful of Reese’s Pieces off the rooftop. The candy smacks the street below like a hard rain. She, more than anyone, is eager to get the radio running and get in touch with other humans.

I suspect Quint feels the same. But Quint—emotionally—he's just sort of *odd*. He has the greatest personality of anyone ever—but he doesn't quite process things like other people.

I mean, Quint's parents are missing, too, like June's. His parents were on vacation when the Monster Apocalypse began. Every time I ask him how he's feeling, how he's doing—y'know, trying to really, like, *connect*—I get nowhere. . . .

So, buddy—I've been meaning to ask. How are you feeling?
I'm feeling like it's time to watch *The Goonies*!

See what I mean?

I look at June. Her head is lowered and her hair is hanging over her face. I hate seeing any of my friends looking so bummed.

So it's time for me—PROTECTOR OF FRIENDS, DEFENDER OF THE REALM, and MASTER, CREATOR, AND KEEPER OF ALL THINGS RADICALLY FUN!—to do my job.

I leap to my feet. "Okay, gang," I say cheerfully. "Quint's going to do some noodling and come up with a plan to get inside so you can find your radio antenna thing. Until then, let's enjoy this day! Hey, June—you want to feed the wild cluckers down by the lake? You always love that."

"No," June says.

"Dance party?" I ask.

"No," June says.

"Hungry Hungry Hippos?" I suggest.

"No," June says.

"Rice Krispies Treat–eating contest?" I offer.

"Jack, stop!" June snaps. "You don't need to make me happy. It's not your job to—"

"Blast the Dirk?" I say.

June's eyes sparkle at that suggestion. Dirk squeals (he does that when he's excited)

Moments later, we're leaping from rooftops, and swinging from lamp posts, back the way we came, eager to get home. . . .

Okay, so . . . Remember I said we nabbed that BallBlaster 2000 from the fancy tennis courts? Well, the *next* thing we did was hoist it up into the tree house and invent a little game called Blast the Dirk.

I grab the machine, and we start blasting. . . .

Right now you might be thinking, wow, this is, like, the meanest, cruelest, straight-up *worst* game I've ever heard of. Blasting your buddy! But it's Dirk's favorite game, too!

See, a few weeks ago, Quint and I dragged Dirk with us to Comically Speaking, my favorite comic book store. Dirk was basically like, "UGH THIS IS ALL DORK STUFF I HATE DORK STUFF I HATE IT HERE."

But then he saw the life-size replica of the Conan the Barbarian sword and he was like, "ACTUALLY THE COMIC BOOK STORE IS THE BEST PLACE AND I ENJOY IT HERE IMMENSELY!"

So Dirk spends every game improving his monster-fighting skills by dodging, spinning, and leaping away from tennis balls—and when he's feeling extra confident, he uses his Conan sword to try to chop the tennis balls right out of the air.

He even dresses up.

Basically, yeah, Dirk—the onetime furiously jerky bully—cosplays Conan the Barbarian.

HA!
Nice try, fools. By Crom, I will defeat all tennis balls!

It is a fantastically fun afternoon. But it's not fun enough to cheer up June entirely. It's not fun enough to keep June from thinking about her family. I start to wonder—is anything?

Could there be some grand, epic, classic, old-fashioned fun out there that's strong enough to keep my friends happy here?

What is that radical and amazing fun?

Does it even exist?

I need to find out—and soon. . . .

Chapter Eight

The more I think about the King Wretch and the dream-vision-thingy, the more I'm supremely freaked. What was the King Wretch trying to show me?

What is it about *me* that got the King Wretch's attention? Why not give June or Dirk or Quint a dream-vision-thingy?

I don't get it! What did I do?! Is it because *I* am the one intended to be the king in this vision of the future? If that *is* the reason, well, I don't know how to feel about that! I don't think I'm particularly kingly or royal, and I don't think I want to be, either! Kings have duties! And I can't even say the word "duties" because it makes me think of "doodies"!

I play a game of Ping-Pong with Rover, hoping it'll let me think clearly. That doesn't work, though, because I end up getting way too into the game. . . .

Quint and Dirk come strolling over, and Quint makes an announcement. "I have drawn up a plan for how we will get into Big Al's Junk Palace so we can retrieve the long-range signal-boosting antenna—"

"And my Helidrone!" I add.

"Yes, yes," Quint says. "And your Helidrone. However, my plan requires a couch. And not just any couch—a *fold-out* couch."

I know exactly where to get one of those: Bardle sleeps on a fold-out couch. Soon . . .

Bardle comes shuffling out of the kitchen. The kitchen is now Bardle's workshop. See, in his *old* world/dimension, Bardle was a conjurer. I think that means "magician," but I've never seen him do any crazy magic—he opened a cage with a wave of his hand once, but that's not exactly Dumbledore-level stuff.

Dirk's already grabbing the couch when Bardle says, "Wait one moment. Jack, is that a large bruise on Rover's side?"

I kneel down beside Rover and run my hand over his side. "Yeah," I say. "It's from a battle we got in with an oversized Winged Wretch."

"Like, whatcha thinkin'?" I ask.

Bardle ponders that for a moment. "Let me handle the Rover issue, because I sense that you, Jack, are already quite full of thought and concern."

Boy, is he ever right: King Wretches, dream-vision-thingies, radios, humans, *everything*.

I would *maybe* tell Bardle how I feel, but not with Dirk around. So I say, "No, no—no concern here. But if you think Rover could use some protection, I won't argue."

Bardle says, "Then I will allow you to borrow my couch on one condition: Dirk, you help me with a Rover-protection project. I don't like the idea of any friendly monster suffering unnecessary pain. Retrieve me some scrap metal, please."

The idea of a "Rover-protection project" sounds pretty kick-butt. Are they gonna, like, *upgrade* my monster-dog? Like a video game? Rover, LEVEL 2. I'm into that!

With that, Dirk and I each lift the couch—and that's when my spinal cord just about snaps like a Twix bar. "Jack!" Dirk barks. "Lift with your legs!"

I groan, reposition myself, and—

Dirk mutters something, and soon he's just carrying the couch outside, single-handedly, over one shoulder.

And that's when I spot it.

On the corkboard on the wall—amid flyers for babysitters, lawn-mowing services, and guitar lessons—is something I've never seen before.

It's a pamphlet for a place called Fun Land.

I pluck it off the board. As I start reading, a smile begins to build and I'm bouncing from foot to foot with excitement. . . .

It's an amusement park! With rides and slides! Coasters and corn dogs!
LAND

It hits me—it's so *obvious*!

If I want to show my friends *maximum fun*, an amusement park is the place to go! I mean, once I show them what it's like to spend a day at this Fun Land joint with *no lines* and *no rules*, there's *no way* they'll still be gung ho about finding other humans and leaving this life behind.

I mean, nobody ever want to an amusement park and had a crummy time! Except for maybe that kid from the movie *Big*—but even he got to be grown up for a while and jump around on a floor piano, and who wouldn't *love* to jump around on some floor pianos?!

I speed out of Joe's Pizza. Dirk's already setting the couch down in front of H&G Supplies, the local hardware joint where he set up a workshop. June and Quint are eyeing the couch.

"Guys, look at this!" I say, waving the pamphlet. "Fun Land! You ever heard of Fun Land? You ever been?"

My buds look at me like I'm crazy for never having heard of the place—like I just ran over and said, "You guys ever heard of a little under-the-radar movie called *Star Wars*?"

Duh, Jack. Fun Land is the greatest! The absolute greatest! No joke!
Nauseating rides aside, it is possibly the most joyous place on Earth.
True facts. That place is dope.

I stare at my friends with dazed disbelief. I'm almost at a loss for words. *Almost*. I exclaim, "HOLD UP, WHAT THE HUH?! IF IT'S SO AWESOME, WHY ARE WE NOT THERE RIGHT NOW? WHY HAVE WE NOT ALREADY GONE MANY MULTIPLE TIMES? WHAT ARE WE WAITING FOR?

June shakes her head. "Jack, it's far away—like, twenty minutes."

"Twenty minutes?" I exclaim, throwing my arms in the air. "Who cares about twenty minutes?! Twenty minutes is nothing! Quint can do an entire crossword puzzle in twenty minutes! Dirk can eat an entire cow in twenty minutes! June probably has a cool twenty-minute thing she can do, too, but I just can't think of it right now 'cause I'm too excited about this amusement park!"

Quint clears his throat. "No, Jack, you don't understand. There's only one way to get there: the *highway*."

Oh.

My shoulders sag. *Crud*.

The highway is bad. Very bad.

Like, *ultimate bad*.

The highway is a post-apocalyptic zombie nightmare straight out of every post-apocalyptic zombie nightmare movie, TV show, comic, video game, *everything*. It's *jam-packed* with rusted, abandoned cars, and every spare inch of road is filled with hungry zombies. We couldn't drive our BoomKarts there, and we *definitely* couldn't take our post-apocalyptic pickup truck, Big Mama.

I feel beaten. Powerless. But only for a moment. I *refuse* to be defeated by a zombie traffic jam. I thrust my chest out and announce, "Then I will come up with a solution! A different way to get there!"

June says, "We can't waste time with amusement parks right now."

"June is correct," Quint says, nodding. "We must put all efforts into finishing the radio."

Of course, *the radio.* The radio that will lead to the end of our time together. Again, it's *always* about the radio.

I fold up the map and put it into my pocket.

This is *not* over.

My buddies' first responses, just a minute earlier—they said it all! Fun Land is the greatest! It's the one thing that's SO FUN that it would change my buds' minds about everything! It's what will keep us here! It's what will make sure the vision comes true!

I dismiss any thoughts of not going. I *will* get us to Fun Land.

For ultimate fun.

For the kind of fun that proves parents aren't necessary, other humans aren't needed, and our post-apocalyptic life is perfect just the way it is.

Chapter Nine

Beyond the Town Square, by the old marsh swamp, is a trio of zombies. They're stuck in the mud, totally unable to move. So Skaelka, Dirk, and I are using them for lasso practice.

I'm terrible at lassoing.

Just then, I hear June calling Dirk and me back to the tree house. We find Quint and June leaning against our post-apocalyptic truck, Big Mama.

Normally, Big Mama is a classic monster-battling vehicle with gadgets and weapons galore. Like this . . .

But not anymore. . . .

Big Mama has *changed*. The bottle-rocket launchers, the arrow turret, the monster-slugging weapons—*everything* that fills the truck bed has been removed.

And been replaced by the couch.

"Um. What am I looking at here?" I ask.

June shrugs. "Quint built it."

Dirk elbows me in the side. "I helped yesterday. But barely."

"Jack, where are the sleeping bags that I requested you retrieve?" Quint asks.

Last week, Quint tasked me with tracking down some heavy-duty, outdoorsy, "I'm about to climb a mountain"–type sleeping bags.

It went well—until I met the zombified staff of Dick's Sporting Goods. . . .

No sleeping bag is worth this!

Anyway, I toss the sleeping bags into Big Mama, and we all climb in. Minutes later, we're pulling up to Big Al's Junk Palace. The zombies are everywhere: surrounding the walls, crowding the gate.

Dirk parks near the fence. The zombies swarm, moaning, pawing at the windows, and generally being gnarly.

June leans forward in her seat. "Quint, how do you plan on getting us inside?"

Quint simply says, "To Big Mama's roof!"

Dirk yanks open the sunroof, and we all clamber up. Looking down at the rotting zombie faces surrounding the truck, I gulp. Their saliva drips and their undead skin stinks. If we fall over the side, we're zombie chow.

"Quint, any chance that whatever we're doing—we could, ah, do it quickly?" I say as a gnarled zombie hand paws at my jeans.

"Moving with haste!" Quint replies as he hops into the truck bed. He gives the couch a final once-over, then turns around and announces, "Friends, meet . . . *the Couch-a-Pult!*"

Um.

We're looking at Bardle's fold-out couch.

I'm not sure how to verbalize my confusion. But, thankfully, June knows *exactly* what to say: *"A COUCH?! This is your solution?! This is how we get inside?! My hot-air balloon idea was better!"*

"My tunnel idea was better!" Dirk says.

"My pogo-stick idea was *not* better," I admit with a shrug. "But still . . . couch-a-pult?"

"Trust me," Quint says, and he tries to say it in a soothing, reassuring sort of way, but it's hard for anything to be soothing or reassuring when there are undead fingers poking at our sneakers. I think one is trying to tie my laces together.

Suddenly, a zombie hand grabs Dirk's shin, and my big bud yells, "Anything's better than zombies!" and then we're all following Dirk's lead, slipping into the sleeping bags, plopping down onto the couch, and squeezing in.

Moments later . . .

"In a moment, we will be launched *over* the wall. When you hit the ground," Quint says, "try to roll."

"Roll?" I ask.

"Correct," Quint says. "To absorb the impact."

"How do I roll? I'm in a sleeping bag. My arms are by my sides."

"Bundle yourself."

"Bundle?" June asks. "How do I *bundle myself*?"

"Just sort of bunch up," Quint says.

"Bunch or bundle?" I ask. "I'm getting mixed messages."

"Bunch," Quint says. "But not too tight, because then the impact might, well, kill you."

"Excuse me?!" June shouts.

"Hold up," I say. "Quint, just how far and high is this going to—ah—*pult* us? Is that a word, 'pult'?"

Quint shrugs. "I haven't actually tested it. . . ."

"You haven't tested it?!" I exclaim. "You're Mr. Sciencey! Isn't testing a big part of science?!"

"June was putting a lot of pressure on me to find a way in here to get the radio antenna!" Quint cries. "And June's a girl."

"What does me being a *girl* have to do with any of it?!" June roars.

"I don't do well under pressure from girls!" Quint says.

"June!" I bark. "What'd you have to go and pressure him for?!"

"I didn't pressure him!" June shoots back. "Besides, I just want to talk to my parents!"

I shake my head. "No one's talking to anyone if this thing catapults—"

"*Couch*-a-pults," Quint corrects me.

"WHATEVER!" I roar. "No one's talking to *anyone* if this thing couch-a-pults us into the side of a building or into a zombie horde."

And then Dirk says, "You guys talk too much," and he reaches down, tugs the fold-out couch lever, and . . .

FLING!

We are launched. Flung upward and propelled forward. We soar over the zombies, over the barbed-wire, into Big Al's Junk Palace, and then—

SMACK!

We slam, full-body blows, into the side of a rusted old minivan, then bounce off and tumble onto the dirt ground.

After some clumsy rolling around, I manage to slip out of the sleeping bag. Standing up, I take in the junkyard—and quickly exclaim, "Yo. Junkyards are *awesome*!"

Most of the lot is filled with broken-down cars with popped hoods and filthy windows. The earth under our feet is hard and dusty. Stacks of tires tower over much of the lot, along with old, rusted machinery. There's a trailer office in the rear.

In the corner of the lot is one massive *towering* skyscraper of a scrap heap. And at the top of that mountain of junk, glistening like a cherry atop a sundae, is my Helidrone!

"Last one to the top of the scrap heap is a rotten—um, well—*they're just rotten*!" I shout, and then we're all racing up the side of the junk heap, scrambling over garbage; it's a Mount Everest made of old refrigerators and tires and car doors.

Pulling myself to the top, I grab the Helidrone. It feels like a Zelda game or something, and I'm Link and I just found, like, an enchanted boomerang. I can practically hear that cool loot-plundering sound effect in my head. . . .

But neither Quint nor June is paying *any* attention to my retrieval enthusiasm, because Quint is holding up a sketch of a long-range signal-boosting antenna. "If we can find this," he says, "the radio will be fully functioning."

June is trembling with anticipation as she and Quint begin searching the junkyard. Dirk, meanwhile, hunts for scrap metal to fulfill his promise to Bardle—his promise to help bring into being *Rover Level 2*.

So I'm left alone.

Alone, but with an entire scrapyard full of vintage cars, rusty appliances, and ancient electronics to do *whatever* I want with. So I say, "How much fun can I have with random junk from the scrapyard?"

The answer is *a lot*.

And the moment my buddies see me having a blast, they get jealous and they drop their little antenna hunt, just like I hoped they would, and we crank the fun-having up to eleven.

June finds a new flagpole spear—the villainous Thrull broke the last one—and that leads to a mega-rad jousting match.

The most peerless and primo of all junkyard games is Surf's Up Scrap Mountain Metal Shredding. Dirk uses his brawny biceps to rip off four old car doors, and we race 'em like surfboards.

Who knew you could have so much fun in a scrapyard?!
Everyone, Jack. **Every**one knew that.

I find a big stack of, like, *ancient* teen magazines. June and I spend hours flipping the old pages, doing quizzes. . . .

The good times come to a screeching halt, however, when Quint calls from an old Volkswagen, "FOUND IT!" He rushes over carrying a small box with a large antenna attached.

June switches gears so quickly I'm surprised she doesn't get whiplash. "Is that really it?" she asks, taking two hesitant steps toward Quint. "That's the long-range signal-boosting antenna?"

Quint nods. "Yes."

June takes a deep breath. She blinks twice. At last, she reaches out for it. "I'll hold on to it," she says. "For safekeeping."

So it's over.

We found what we came for.

Our day at Big Al's Junk Palace is done. And I really don't want it to be done. Everything right now just feels *right*.

So I make a proposal. . . .

"Guys," I say. "I'm in no mood to make the leap back to Big Mama. So I was thinking . . ."

YES! Proposal approved in a 4–0 landside!

A first-rate sleepover requires first-rate cuisine, so I search Big Al's shack office for munchable dinner-type stuff that isn't lousy. Dirk gets a tiny fire going, and soon we're cooking up some very decent makeshift s'mores made from stale Pop-Tarts, hot chocolate mix, and Cool Whip.

The sun is way past set when we head to bed.

One problem: the flesh-fiending moan of the zombies is not a great sleeping soundtrack; plus, I have this awful image in my head of the zombies pushing down the fence and devouring us while we snooze.

So we scale the scrap mountain, out of the zombies' reach, and settle into cozy bedtime spots.

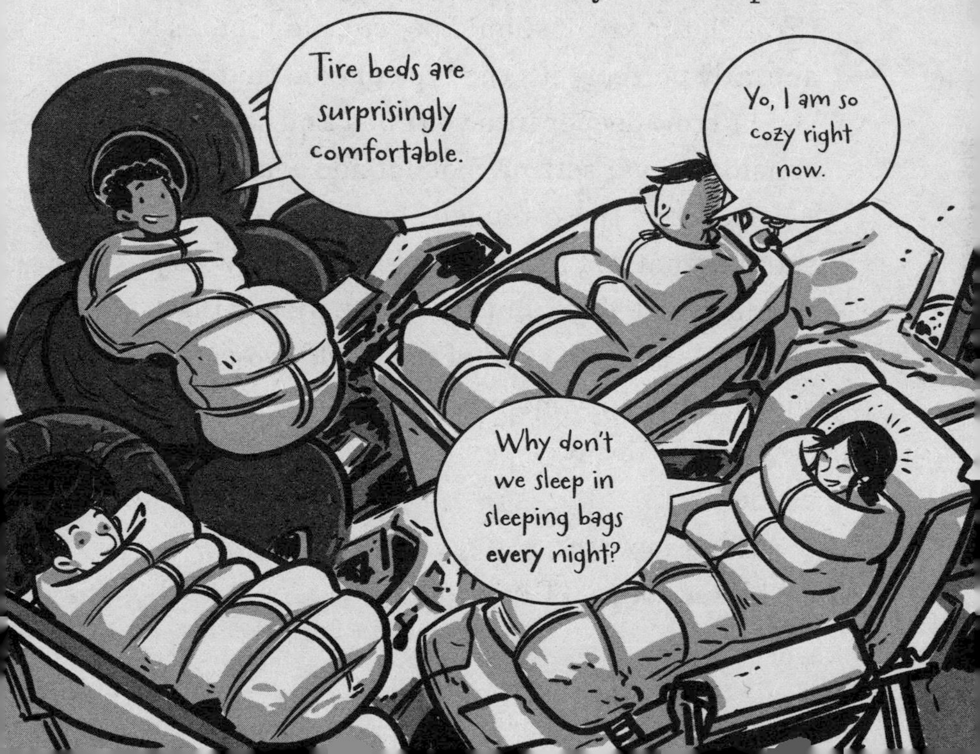

We talk for hours: inane conversations and absurd discussions. And the entire time, no one talks about the radio. No one talks about the fact that Quint finally has what he needs to complete it. That blasted phrase "long-range signal-boosting antenna" is not uttered even once.

The hard truth for me? In just a few days my friends will be able to get in touch with other humans. But no one brings that up. And that makes me happiest of all.

Dirk begins snoring first. And then Quint.

I pull the sleeping bag a bit tighter around me. The nights are growing colder, and a chill slices through the air. It should be *too* cold, but it's actually perfect—it's the type of cold that makes you burrow deeper into your bed and seriously consider never setting foot outside again.

It's one of those snuggly, burrowed-up snoozes that you usually only get on snow days and fake sick days. But that's one nice thing about life after the end of the world: you get to share quiet, cozy moments with pals.

"June?" I say, whispering her name. "You still awake?"

After a moment, she says quietly, "Yep."

"I liked today. I like right now."

"Mmm-hmm," she says.

"This feels like—like this—this might be—" I stop myself, not sure I want to finish. I clear my throat, and continue. "I feel like this might have been the best day of my life."

Quiet, for a moment, and then June says, "For real?"

"I think so, yeah. Riding around in a post-apocalyptic truck, using silly gadgets, playing junkyard games, exploring—and doing it all with my best friends. And then talking all night, by a fire, even, with s'mores! I know it's super lame—but I *loved* that."

"Not lame."

"What was your favorite day?" I ask. "Y'know. Since everything . . ."

"Honestly?"

"Honestly."

June takes her time before she answers. "It was when we heard the voices on the radio—when I realized there was still hope."

She turns, craning her neck to look up at me. I can just barely make out her face in the yellow moonlight. "But today was fun, too! And the day you came to the school."

"Ha. To 'rescue' you?"

"Yeah, to 'rescue' me."

I think back to that day, months earlier, and laugh at my lousy rescue attempt—and what it taught me about damsels in distress. . . .

I chuckle. And there's silence for a bit longer. The only sound is the moaning zombies.

And lying there, at the top of a giant scrap heap, surrounded by zombies, in this weirdest of weird situations, I finally have the courage to say what I've been feeling. . . .

"June, when you guys complete the radio, you'll get in touch with other humans. Maybe even your parents. Then our group—our team—it'll never be the same again. We'll probably get split up. Forever."

As I'm saying it out loud, it hits me full on like a freight train of feeling—and I practically puke. Monsters are scary. But for me—for a kid who spent his whole life wanting friends and then finally got them—monsters aren't *nearly* as scary as the idea of your friends going away.

"June?" I whisper. "Did you hear what I said?"

And then I hear her snoring gently. . . .

I like the way her snoring sounds.

I reach into my pocket and unfold the Fun Land map. I don't try to wake June up. I only say softly, "I'd just really like to get to Fun Land before we're split up. And ride this thing—the Thunder Coaster. I've never ridden a roller coaster before. If we're all going to get split up, I think this would be a good last hurrah."

And then I drift off to sleep, too.

But I'm not asleep for long. . . .

Chapter Ten

I sit up, startled, not feeling right.

I feel movement. Like I'm on a waterbed, I think. Of course I've never *been* on a waterbed because waterbeds are for cool dudes.

"Dirk?" I groan, groggy. "Is that you moving around? I'm trying to sleep."

Dirk's only response is a nasty, phlegmy snore-snort.

And then I smell something like gym socks slathered with buffalo wing sauce.

"Dirk!" I bark, sitting up. "Did you let one rip in your sleep?"

I'm about to give him major grief—or maybe compliment him on the stunningly powerful odor he emitted—when I realize it's a different smell. Not like anything I've smelled before.

It's not evil.

But it is monstrous. . . .

My stomach rolls and my wheelbarrow bed shifts and squeaks. I'm suddenly feeling not so great about our situation. I crawl out of my sleeping bag and start down the scrap mountain.

But then—

SNAP!

My foot punches through a splintered piece of wood. I pull my sneaker back, but it's sort of stuck, like I stepped on a pile of Elmer's glue or something.

Finally freeing it, I push the scrap aside and peer through the hole. Something is glowing: a yellow-orange color.

I press my eye closer, and then—

I topple back. Then I'm suddenly sliding down a scrap avalanche! I tumble into Quint, saying, "Wake up, wake up, wake up."

"Huh?" Quint says.

"WAKE. UP," I say, wanting to shout but trying to whisper. "This isn't just a pile of junk we're on."

"What's happening?" June asks, all dazed. "I was having the best dream. I had a phone again and I was texting. . . . Emoji heaven . . ."

Dirk's already up. He's realizing what I'm realizing. He stuffs the scraps he gathered for Bardle into his sleeping bag.

June grabs her new flagpole spear. I'm about to shout, "NO!" but it's too late. She's pushing the spear down into the junk, using it to get to her feet. I hear a *SPURT* as the sharp tip hits *whatever* is beneath us and—

GRAWWRRRRR!

Guys. This isn't just a scrap heap.
It's something else. Something we **didn't** invite to our sleepover.

"Like an annoying little sister?" Quint asks. I swear, this kid—it takes him longer than anyone to get his head together when he wakes up.

The junk rocks, everything beneath our feet sliding and quaking and shifting. "No, Quint, not like an annoying little sister! Like . . ."

The scrap mountain EXPLODES from the inside out, and we're flung to the hard dirt ground. We scramble across the lot, diving for cover behind a heaping pile of tires.

"What is that thing?" June says, gasping.

"It's big," Dirk says. "That's what it is."

I pull the Louisville Slicer from its sheath. Staying low, I wriggle on my belly toward Quint. Together, we peek around the tire mound—and we gasp in horror. . . .

"It's like the Kraken," Quint whispers.

"The Kraken is a water monster," I say. "Come

on—how many times did we watch *Pirates of the Caribbean* together?"

"Perhaps it's an aboveground Kraken," Quint suggests.

"No such thing as an aboveground Kraken," I say.

This tentacle-covered horror defies description: it's monstracious, gigantesque, terrifiable. The monster writhes, its tentacles toss aside trash, and we see the full, terrifying, bloodcurdling breadth of the beast.

Quint stammers: "It's—it's—it's—it's—"

"I know what it is," I say. "It's like . . ."

-The Scrapken!-
One eye—which is one too many.
"Just woke up" face.

Rotten, chewed-up Dozer flesh.
Snapping, cracking tentacles.
General aura of ferocity.

"The Scrapken?!" Quint exclaims. "The Scrapken is a terrible name for a monster! It sounds like 'scrappy napkin'!"

"You got a better name?" I demand.

"Well, no, I suppose I don't," Quint admits. "Not off the top of my head. But of course, properly naming a monster requires serious thought and study and—"

"No more monster-name talk!" Dirk barks, yanking us back behind the tire pile.

I shrug. "Sure, fine, less worrying about names and more worrying about how we *give this guy the business*. And by give this guy the business, I mean teach him all about my professional occupation—aka *business*—which is MONSTER-STOMPING POST-APOCALYPTIC HERO!"

"Or we could just leave," June suggests.

Oh. Right. Duh. This monster isn't evil—he's just, like, super protective of his home, which is fine, totally get that. If some strangers started randomly napping on top of our tree house, I'd be all like, "Eat this fist!"

"Fine," I say, "Then let's give this guy the business, and by give this guy the business, I mean flee in fear—which is *not* my professional occupation but which *is* something I will do now!"

Peeking through the rubber, I spot Big Al's office trailer. If we can get to the roof, then we could leap over the fence and—as long as we don't get zombie-eaten—make it to Big Mama.

I scramble from beneath the tires. "Follow me!"

We're racing toward the trailer, sneakers pounding scrap, when . . .

My getaway route is demolished with one tentacle whack! The monster howls, and then we're spinning, running the other way, dodging and diving. Tentacles pound, punch, and pummel the ground around us.

One tentacle hits a rusty vending machine, smashing it in half. Suddenly, an idea!

"We need to make one of the tentacles smack the big wall!" I shout. "The Scrapken can knock us a way out of here!"

Quint opens his mouth to argue, but a tentacle nearly takes his head off and he shuts right up.

We race to the wall. On the other side is an army of zombies and our means of escape: Big Mama.

We stand like statues.

The easiest possible target.

"Over here, Scrapken!" I shout. "Come hit us!"

"Yeah!" Quint hollers. "We're awaiting a whacking! Eager, even!"

We look up as one thick, wet tentacle lifts. Watching this massive flesh bat about to maybe smash us has my heart doing backflips.

"This better work. . . ." Dirk says.

"If it doesn't," June says, "we're all going to—"

"DIVE!" I shout, and we all leap just as . . .

WALL WALLOP!

The wall falls, and the zombies are instantly rushing in, shambling over the broken brick. Thankfully, the next tentacle swing slams into a tire pile, and about nine hundred ninety-nine pounds of rubber plow into the zombies. Some are knocked aside, and others are sent pinwheeling through the air.

Through the shattered wall, I glimpse Big Mama. *"Go, go, go!"* I order.

"Wait!" June screams. Her eyes are darting around. "The antenna! I don't have it!"

I hesitate for a second. We could let the antenna go. Let it be lost. And then I wouldn't have to worry about them leaving. At least not for a long while.

It's like a gift from the monster gods!

Should I?

Could I?

No . . . I cannot!

"Where is it?" I bark.

June's voice cracks as she cries, "I don't know! It was with me on top of the junk heap!"

We gaze out at the scrapyard, eyes darting and searching like it's the highest-stakes hidden-object game of all time—and at last, June points—"THERE!"

I see it. Laying on the ground, amid the other scattered trash.

"You guys go," I say. "I'll get it."

"What?" Quint exclaims. "Jack! No!"

But I'm already rushing back into the scrapyard. A tentacle CRASHES down behind me and cuts me off from my friends. Another tentacle screams toward me, but I reach out, lunging, and . . .

THWACK!
I hate you, antenna—but I got you!

I scramble to my feet, turning back, eyeing the broken-wall exit. Zombies are pouring through. A tentacle swings toward me, and I *dive* inside the closest cover: a gas-guzzling old junker. Metal crunches as the tentacle throttles the trunk. The stink of motor oil and grease is suffocating.

"Stop, Scrapken!" I holler through the car's cracked windshield. "Listen to me! You're not evil! Just be cool! I'll leave if you let me!"

MOOOOOANNNNN!

The zombies have my scent. They're staggering toward me. Crud!

My eyes dart around the car, looking for the keys. But then I realize, with an audible *gulp*, that the car has no hood and *no engine*.

I frantically start rolling up the window—but I'm too slow. A rotting zombie hand swipes at me! Another grabs my sleeve!

I hurl my body to the side, but my evasive maneuver fails. The undead brutes are all around me! Snatching and grabbing from all directions!

The zombies are at every window, crawling into the car, but then—

WHACK!

A tentacle pounds the roof. The car shakes and the zombies are hurled back.

I've been saved—but only for a moment.

A Scrapken tentacle shoots through the air, slaps the roof, then surrounds the car. It's choking the metal frame like an anaconda—tightening and squeezing and crushing! The ceiling crumples. The doors crack!

And then the car is lifted—*I'm* lifted—into the air. There's a little hula dancer on the dashboard and she's rocking back and forth like it's a midnight dance party.

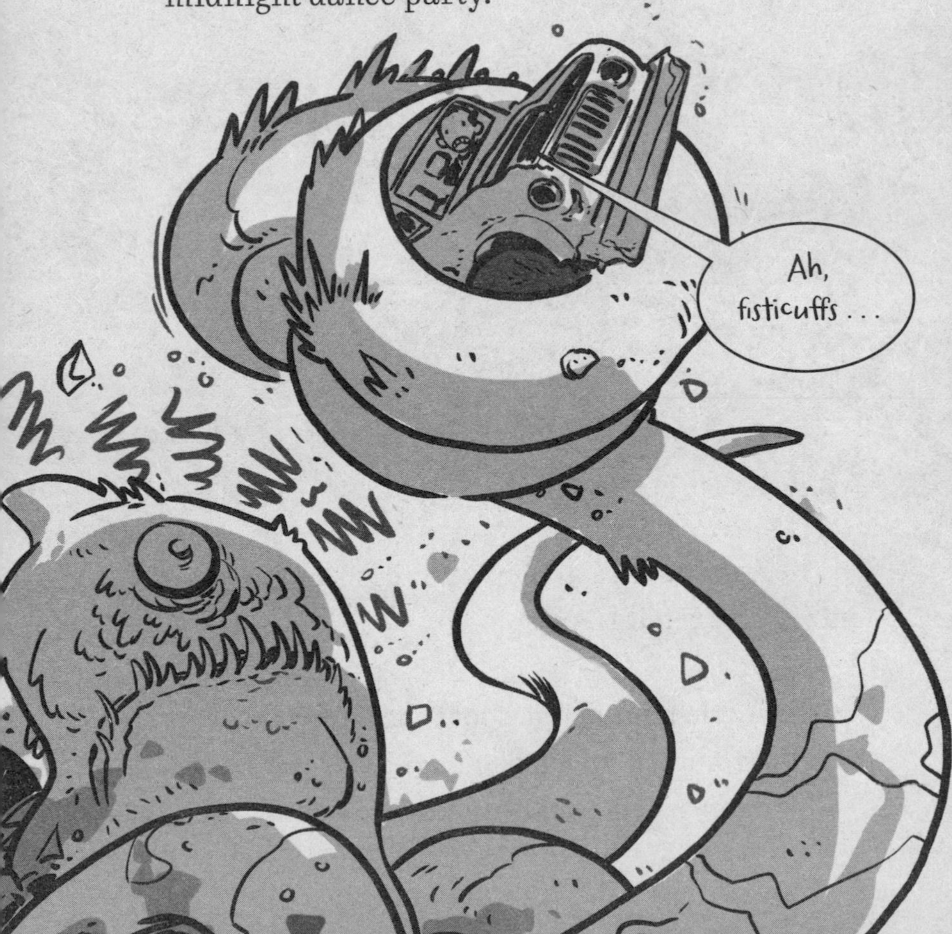

There's zero chance this ends gently.

I tug on the seat belt, but it's stuck. The car lurches. The hula dancer on the dash is shaking her hips like there's no tomorrow—and if I don't get this seat belt on, there might *not* be a tomorrow.

"Come on, stupid seat belt!" I cry, pulling harder.

The tentacle squeezes, the metal moans, and I'm hoisted higher. The car tilts and flips. My head meets the armrest. The hula girl is moving and grooving. Then my head slams against the steering wheel, and I just *know* that's going to bruise.

I'm tugging, grasping at the seat belt, pulling and yanking, and then it finally budges, and I'm stabbing the buckle into the slot, slamming it, and at the last possible second, I hear a CLICK, and then—

So I'm flying through the air.

That's bad.

But on the plus side, hey, it's one way to escape a junkyard! As the car spins, I catch a quick glimpse of the junk monster slipping back beneath the ground, the scrap again piling on top of him.

And as the car flips and plummets, the only thing I'm thinking is, "Man, I really hope this thing has airbags."

BOOM!

The car crashes to the street, a block from Big Al's, then slides and skitters another full block, tumbling and rolling and yes the car does have airbags and yes they do work and WOW airbags *hurt* as they punch me in the face, but . . .

I'M ALIVE!

"Hula girl, we made it!" I exclaim. And then I realize I'm talking to an inanimate dashboard doll.

I crawl from the wreckage. Dazed, woozy, I manage to stand. Aches and pains and bruises, but nothing major. I scoop up the radio antenna.

"Dudes?" I call out. "Dudes, where are you?"

I hear no dudes.

But I do hear something else.

A Dozer. It must have heard the action.

I haven't even *started* recovering from the whole flying, flipping car thing—and now this stony colossus is *charging* toward me. . . .

But then—a high-pitched squeal! Big Mama is screeching to a halt. "Jack, get in!" June shouts as she flings the door open.

And I do.

I sprint, dive inside, and then we're speeding away—leaving the Dozer in the dust.

For a moment, no one says anything.

And then . . .

Chapter Eleven

I'm on breakfast duty. Our grill is on the fritz, so I'm using the BoomKart engine to sizzle up some hearty breakfast sandwiches: grilled Twinkies stuffed with sizzling Lucky Charms.

"Jack!" Quint calls from the tree house. "Come here! No delay!"

I dump the food on a dish—we found this fancy china platter at some old lady zombie's house, and it makes every meal Queen of England–level classy.

"Rover, go visit Bardle for a bit, okay?" I say. He scampers off, and I balance the platter like an expert waiter as I make my way up into the tree house.

But as soon as I enter, I lose my appetite. . . .

Gulp. Drat. Crud.

Okay, Jack, stay calm.

I feel that hot panicky-ness coming over me again. I remind myself this is a good thing—my friends are *happy*. But still, I can barely breathe. Hard to breathe. Can't breathe. Not sure what to say, I just blurt out, "I MADE BREAKFAST!"

Dirk's eyes light up. He yanks the platter from my hands and chomps on a Twinkie sandwich while Quint dives into a rapid-fire presentation.

"Jack, perhaps best of all, the radio is PORTABLE! It fits right inside this backpack. No matter where we are, we need never risk missing a radio call."

June steps toward me. "Jack, this might all be over soon."

Okay, I was maintaining control; I really was. But now my heart is thumping, slamming, pounding. I need to get out of this tree house before my heart *detonates*. I need an excuse to leave, any excuse, just something—

No.

No.

WAIT!

What I *actually* need to do is NOT GIVE UP. If I show my buds THE MOST FUN EVER, then maybe—*maybe, maybe, maybe*—there's still a chance they won't want to leave. It just needs to be fun ENOUGH.

The sleepover at the junkyard wasn't fun enough.

Blast the Dirk isn't fun enough.

Human-monster games weren't fun enough.

The Streets Are Lava isn't fun enough.

But I still believe the funnest of all fun things could change their minds! This is it. My last shot. So . . .

"Leave the big plans to me," I say.

I grab a Twinkie sandwich and reach for the zip line. "Trust me. I got this, guys! I *totally* got this."

I don't got this. Not at all.

I mean, look, I know what we have to do. If we're talking CRAZY, COOL CELEBRATION and if we're talking MOST FUN EVER, there's really only one proper way to do that.

FUN LAND!

My buddies said it themselves, not long ago. . . .

Duh, Jack. Fun Land is the greatest! The absolute greatest! No joke!
Nauseating rides aside, it is possibly the most joyous place on Earth.
True facts. That place is dope.

But how?

The highway is chockablock full of abandoned cars and zombies and is *totally* impassable. Big Mama can't get there, BoomKarts can't get there, and we can't walk. . . .

ARGH! Think, Jack, think! You can figure this out!

There's something about needing to fix everything right this moment that makes it so hard to think clearly! I've got my head down, walking through the Town Square, mind racing, when—

SMACK!

I walk headlong into Biggun. My nose collides with his bony knee.

Sorry, I didn't see you there.
And, yes, I realize how absurd that sounds.

Biggun stoops down and sniffs my Twinkie-and-Lucky-Charms sammie. "Um. Go ahead, buddy, all yours," I say, holding it out. Biggun's massive paw scoops up the sandwich, and he plops down on the sidewalk. It's an earthshaking power plop. I sit beside him and watch him enjoy my fine cooking.

Just then, my eyes are drawn to something. The soles of Biggun's feet—they're made of, like, bone or something.

"Biggun, are you, uh—ticklish?" I ask.

Biggun's only response is a grunt. I'm hoping that grunt means no, because I lean forward and knock three times on the sole of his left foot. It's hard. Very hard.

An idea is beginning to form. . . .

I think back to our Monsters Versus Humans Almighty Ultra-Important Tournament Games and how Biggun completely dominated the Tug-of-War with his ridiculous strength. And I remember seeing Biggun lifting, like, six of the monsters up on his shoulders as they celebrated their big win.

"Biggun," I say, "I could *really* use your help. Wanna go for a walk? A kind of long walk?"

"Grr-unt?"

"Grr-unt is right. C'mon, follow me."

I pull my walkie from my pocket. *"Jack to tree house. Dirk, do me a solid and meet me at the hardware store in, say, four minutes. Over, out, all that copy, roger, 10-4 stuff."*

Four minutes later, I'm outside the hardware store, saying to Dirk, "We're going to build something. Something big. Something for this guy."

Biggun is standing beside me.

While Dirk looks the huge monster up and down, I find a pen and quickly sketch on the back of the Fun Land park map. When I finish, Dirk examines my drawing. "Really?" he asks.

I nod.

Then he looks up at Biggun. Again, he says, *"Really?"*

Biggun shrugs.

"Okay then," Dirk says. And with that, the project is under way. . . .

You know you're insane, right?
But good insane, I think! A solid sorta insane!

I try to help Dirk, but I'm pretty much 100 percent useless. First, I hit my thumb with a hammer. Then, I lose control of the hammer, it flies from my hand, and it nearly knocks Dirk in the skull. When it comes to building stuff, I'm a hopelessly incompetent and incapable louse. I'm doing more bad than good, so I plop down on a nearby truck that Biggun is using as a seat.

"Jack," Dirk says, "you want to make yourself useful?"

"Is that a rhetorical question? 'Cause I'm pretty comfy here. Sun's out, enjoying a cool beverage, feeling—"

Dirk glares, hard, then cracks his knuckles.

I grin. "I'd be delighted to help! What can I do?"

"I need two shopping carts to build the base of this ridiculous contraption. Get me those; I can finish."

I leap down off the truck and exclaim, "In that case, I'm on it! Next stop: Atlantic Supermarket!"

"Take someone with you!" Dirk calls.

"Nah. Going solo!" I call back. "I got the Louisville Slicer. What could go wrong?"

Chapter Twelve

Atlantic Supermarket is about a mile from the Town Square, but it's worth the journey because the shopping carts are enormous.

I'm following one of our usual The Streets Are Lava routes. I make quick progress, moving from the Taco Bell to the bank, then swinging from Dandelion's Ice Cream to the post office.

Usually me and my buds would all work together to make it across—but now I'm playing solo.

And that's good—it's important I learn to do things alone, since once that radio starts doing radio things, who knows what the future holds? I might be doing *a lot* of things by myself.

Things like swinging from lampposts and landing totally awesomely like Spider-Man . . .

I make it—*painfully*—to the roof of Atlantic Supermarket. I glance over the side and see zombies galore pawing at the doors. No problem—I'll grab the carts, leave out the back, and speed all the way home.

I snap open the roof's access panel and slip inside like a post-apocalyptic cat burglar.

The store has been picked over. The aisles are littered with microwave popcorn kernels and rotting fruit, and the store stinks of spoiled milk. The odor is overpowering—thankfully, I quickly find two shopping carts. I'm pushing them toward a rear exit when I pass a towering shelf loaded with Capri Sun.

Capri Sun is *just* what I've been craving since my first radio panic moment.

At the very top is my favorite flavor: Pacific Cooler. I scramble up, unable to resist.

But as I leap down, there's a sudden SNAP! I tumble back—the huge shelf is falling!

It topples into the next, like dominos, one by one, until the final shelf CRASHES through the front doors.

Oh no.

Not good.

The front door was keeping the zombies out. And I just put a shelf *through* theat front door!

There's a tremendous howl as a hundred undead mouths open wide. The horde lurches and shambles through the door. Snarling, hands raised, charging toward me.

I swallow hard and pull out the Louisville Slicer. It will be just me against hundreds of rotting monsters, but at least I'll go down fighting.

But then I hear the thunderclap. The beating of wings. The King Wretch.

With one massive, snapping *chomp*, the King Wretch devours a dozen zombies. A simple swallow, sucking them down. He grabs another dozen, chomping them like a T. rex, then swinging his neck and hurling them through the door.

Wait . . .

Is he . . .

Is he *saving* me?

The heavy stench of evil in the air sends the remaining zombies shuffling away in fear. The King Wretch squeezes into the store. Bony wings shred the ceiling as the monster stomps toward me.

But this time, the King Wretch doesn't just stare at me. . . .

His talons punch me square in the chest. I hit the cold floor and the claws tighten, digging into my shoulders. Hot saliva drips from the King Wretch's fangs and splashes against my cheek. The monster's eyes are swirling pits of darkness, and they draw me in. I can almost hear some goofy hypnotist saying, "You're getting very sleepy. . . ."

Because that's what's happening.

All sound fades.

The eyes. The eyes of the King Wretch are snapping and flashing like lightning—and I can't pull myself away. I hear one sound.

A sound *inside* my head: a BOOM, and I'm suddenly transported.

I'm in the Town Square, again.

The air stinks of evil and foulness. I taste something tart on my tongue, like milk gone bad.

The town is empty. Abandoned.

Everyone seems to have vanished. Zombies moan and shamble past me.

I push open the door and enter Joe's Pizza.

A sour smell hits me. And then I see the awfulness. My legs tremble. My brain, my thoughts—they flicker.

I snap my eyes shut. I can't look. I won't.

But the image is still there, behind my eyelids. . . .

The monsters. . . . My friends. . . . They've been . . . destroyed. . . .

Bits and pieces of armor are scattered about. Green slime drips from the walls and the tables and *everything*. I retreat back outside.

Spinning, I see the buildings have been leveled, razed, nearly all of them. In the distance are plumes of black smoke.

Last time, the dream was *good*. But this is the exact opposite.

This is a nightmare. I don't understand.

In the dream, I shout, "KING WRETCH! WHY ARE YOU DOING THIS?! WHAT DO YOU WANT???"

But I get no answer.

The odor of smoke grows stronger, and that's when I see the tree house.

Our home.
It's burning.

I hurry toward it. I climb the ladder.
Fire licks my face, but I don't feel it.
My friends. They're inside. I know it.
I call their names, but I get nothing.

Oh no.

Oh no.

Oh no . . .

This is the pinnacle of all nightmares. It is the type of terror that breaks you. And as I push open the door, I swallow. I'm not ready for what I'm about to see. . . .

Skaelka yanks me free! I'm instantly snapped out of the nightmare. The King Wretch snarls, but Skaelka raises her razor-sharp ax and steps forward. "Leave, demon!" she barks. "Leave while you are still able!"

The King Wretch's eyes are no longer swirling, mystical things. But there is anger in those eyes. Whatever the monster was trying to show me was interrupted—and he is not pleased.

The King Wretch glares a final time, then stomps out of the store. His wings beat, and he shoots into the sky.

"Are you alive?" Skaelka asks.

"Yes, I think so," I say. "And, hey, I appreciate the rescue—but why are you here?"

"Followed you."

"Why?"

"I thought maybe your brain broke again. I thought I might need to perform the dance of decapitation on you."

"My brain's fine," I say, although that is a *total and complete lie*. I'm beyond freaked out by that nightmare the King Wretch just dragged me through. But I'm trying not to show it. I don't want to give Skaelka any reason to think she needs to do a decapitation dance.

My palms are dripping sweat. I wipe them on my jeans and try to put on a normal face. "Hey, Skaelka—don't tell my friends what happened, okay?"

Skaelka nods.

"You mind pushing one of these?" I say as I grab the shopping carts. And with that, we make our way home, together.

Back in the Town Square, I say good-bye to Skaelka then walk to the hardware store. I see Dirk's almost done. "Any problems?" Dirk asks.

"Nope!" I lie. "Easy-peasy."

"Good," Dirk says. He grabs a giant hacksaw and begins sawing at the carts.

I sit down and shut my eyes, trying to wrap my head around what happened at the supermarket. The first dream-vision-thingy: it was weird, but it wasn't *bad*. In fact, I thought it was *good*!

But now I've been given *two* dream-vision-thingies. And that last one? It wasn't a dream at all. It was a legit NIGHTMARE. I can't knock those awful images from my head: my friends, the monsters, everyone suffering.

That first vision—I thought it was like a real-deal accurate prediction of the future. But now I know that's not true. It was something else. The King Wretch is playing around inside my head.

But why?

I must get answers from the King Wretch. I must—I *will*—do whatever it takes to make sure what I saw in that nightmare never comes true.

Suddenly, Dirk's shaking me. "All finished," he says. "And Biggun's ready to go."

I rub at my eyes. My mouth is dry and my body is drained. I'm so completely freaked that I don't even feel like going to Fun Land right now—but if I want to keep my friends, I can't delay.

I drag my butt over to Biggun. I ask, "You up for a run, big fella?"

"GRRRRUNT."

"Right on, my man."

And so, minutes later . . .

June and Quint appear on the tree house deck—and their eyes just about pop out of their sockets.

"What strange lunacy is this?" Quint asks.

I flash a slick smile. "This is . . ."

–The Biggun Mobile!–

I hold up a hand. "And before you start to protest, saying, 'Oh, it's too dangerous! Oh, it will take too long! Oh, I don't have anything to wear'—*and yes, Quint, I'm talking to you!* Just listen, guys. Biggun is crazy fast and his monster feet can stomp over anything."

"But the radio—" June starts.

Before she can finish, I say: "And, June, like you said, you can take your radio with you. It's totally portable."

June purses her lips and glances hesitantly at Quint. Quint looks at me and sees the thing that, sometimes, only a *best friend* can see: the supreme significance of something to that friend. He sees just how totally important this is to me—even if he doesn't know *why*.

Quint grins. "I'm in."

"Okay then," June says. She slings the radio backpack over her shoulder, hops the tree house railing, and drops into my cart. Quint follows, sidling up beside Dirk.

And we're off.

Chapter Thirteen

Cars, trucks, and bad-to-the-bone Harley Davidsons are *crushed* beneath Biggun's feet. Zombies moan with frustrated hunger as we speed past. Biggun is in, like, *dash mode* the entire journey.

"Look!" Quint says, pointing as we round a bend.

I see the top of the Ferris wheel. And then the peak of the Thunder Coaster. I can imagine what a sight Fun Land would be, all lit up on a summer night—lights radiating for miles and miles. A beacon calling out, saying, "Laughter and good times for all—RIGHT HERE!"

But there's none of that now—and that's okay. This, to me, is perfect.

"I can't believe you did so much just to get us here," June says with a hint of wonder in her voice. "You're a good friend, Jack."

I just shrug and force a half smile, because I'm not sure how true that is.

CRUNCH! Biggun yanks the front gate away, then we all hop down. We step over the crumpled gate, and we're there, *inside* Fun Land. We have made it. I let out a soft long, carefree whistle. . . .

"So, what are we going to ride first?" I ask, rubbing my hands together.

"First?" Dirk asks. "First we should probably figure out what to do with this guy." He hooks a a thumb at Biggun.

Biggun answers that question himself. He's stomping toward a food stand. His hand slams through the wall and he yanks out a thick wad of cotton candy. I choke back a barf as I watch roaches crawl over the sticky pink treat.

It's less than appetizing, but Biggin gulps it down and shoves his hand back in for more.

"Y'know," I say. "I think he might be good here for a while. . . ."

"OKAY! NO MORE DELAYS! Let the good times roll! And bounce! Or just, y'know, flow. Whatever the good times wanna do, they can do," I say.

"Jack, just one more holdup. . . ." Quint says.

ARGH! WHY ARE THERE SO MANY HOLDUPS!? It's like a bank robber convention!

Quint points out that there's no electricity in the park. But Dirk quickly finds a little shack of a building with the words "ELECTRICAL MAINTENANCE" on the door.

Inside, Dirk yanks a series of grease-slick levers. Soon, an electrical *HUMMMMMMM* begins to fill the park.

Fun Land is turning on: all of it coming to life, magical wonder in the air. Rides whir, lights flash, music plays, and I'm filled with a warm maple syrup feeling that's just *joy*.

Guys . . . ultimate fun . . . has begun. . . .

We laugh and joke and tease. Each of my friends wears a smile bigger than I've seen *in months*.

I completed my goal: I have delivered *ULTIMATE FUN!*

Like I said, this is my first amusement park *ever*—but it takes me only like six minutes to announce, "I AM NOW EXTREMELY IN LOVE WITH AMUSEMENT PARKS! The guy who invented them deserves his own holiday! I mean,

if the world ever gets back to normal and there actually *are* holidays again."

"The *guy* who invented amusement parks?" June says, jabbing me in the side. "It could have been a girl. A *woman*."

"Yes! Of course! Duh!" I reply. "Totally smart and accurate point. Whichever woman or man or kid or dude or *what* invented amusement parks—they are a world hero."

Each ride is more awesome than the last—except for a few where we find monsters lurking in unexpected places . . . Like the Paratrooper . . .

After that, we practically puke on the Flying Scooters, and then the Matterhorn whips us, the Gravitron spins us, and the Pirate Ship flips us. And by the time we stumble off the Round Up . . .

"I'm going to vomit," Quint moans.

"Let's do it again!" June exclaims.

MURGHHHH!!!! GRRUUUUARNN!

A zombie moan cuts through the air. Nothing ruins a pleasant afternoon like a zombie moan.

But it's all good! The few zombies in the park are stuck inside game booths. They wear matching red-and-white Fun Land uniforms. It would maybe even be cute, if their faces weren't falling off their skulls.

Ignoring the zombies, Quint and Dirk spot the High-Strike—leading to the most lopsided game ever. . . .

For a moment, it's just June and me, alone. I want to ask her something, but it's like I can't speak. Talking to June all buddy-buddy is no problem, but this is different—the words just won't come out of my mouth. I'd *jam* my arm down my throat and *yank* the words out if I could—but then the words would be covered in slobber and, really, who wants slobber words? No one wants slobber words, that's who.

Finally, I manage to mumble, "June, can I win you a prize?"

"Whaddya mean?" June says.

"You know. Like in a movie! Where the boy proves he's the coolest by winning the girl a giant stuffed Smurf or some junk at a carnival game!"

June wrinkles her nose. "Um, how about . . . NO? More like *I'd* be winning *you* a prize."

"Oh. Even better!" I say, grinning. "You said it—*you* gotta win *me* a prize. And you can't just yank some junk from a booth! You have to actually *win it*—playing by the rules."

June crosses her arms, thinks on that for a second, and then nods. "Challenge accepted!"

And with that—the zombie carnival games begin . . .

Super Sweet and Lighthearted Fun Land Sequence!

June finally triumphs in a game of Rootin' Tootin' Shootin' in the park's Wild West Land. "Okay, little Jack," she says, using a total mom voice. She even musses my hair and asks, "Which prize would you like, honey?"

She's 100 percent making fun of me, but I don't care; I just like hearing her call me honey—it makes my belly region warm.

"The sheriff's cowboy hat thing!" I say, pointing to one of the many Wild West–type prizes. "I'll give it to Dirk, since he's all into cowboy stuff."

June avoids the zombie varmint behind the counter and plucks the cowboy hat from the prize wall. I grasp the hat—and for a brief moment, we're both holding it.

For that brief moment, I don't have a care in this undead world. For that brief moment, life is perfection.

But like I said, it's a brief moment. . . .

Quint and Dirk come around the corner. I see the radio antenna jutting out of Quint's backpack, bobbing and swaying with each step.

And it happens.

A light flashes on the radio. Next is

a cracking, hissing sound. The radio is broadcasting. . . .

"*STATIC, CRACKLE*—OUR NEXT BROADCAST WILL BE OUR FINAL BROADCAST—*STATIC, CRACKLE*—IS ANYONE THERE?—*STATIC, CRACKLE*—"

June gasps. The cowboy hat drops from her hand. She darts toward Quint and the radio.

And just like that, I'm forgotten.

Even this, *the perfect moment*, can't hold a candle or a lantern or a flashlight or *whatever* to their precious, stupid, special, might-as-well-be-freaking-magic *radio*!

We're surrounded by roller coasters and games, and they'd rather spend their time with strangers on a radio. They'd rather listen to strangers than have fun with me.

I really believed Fun Land was the one thing that could change their minds. The one thing that could prove that this life we've created here is *worth not leaving behind*.

But I was wrong.

Nothing can.

And that realization—it causes me to, well, kind of lose it. . . .

I'm heaving. My body is trembling. My muscles—my dinky little muscles—are clenched tight.

My friends look away from the radio. They watch me. They're silent. A little scared, even.

I'm suddenly overcome, half-deranged, and I'm racing toward them. Quint's eyes go wide and he stammers, “Hey, hey, wait, friend! What are you doing?!”

“I’m destroying THIS AWFUL THING!” I screech. I rip the radio from Quint’s hands and lift it radio high above my head.

A crazy Gollum-type madness surges through me. I’m practically giggling like a lunatic. I’m going to *smash* it against the hard concrete. But I don’t.

I can’t.

Not with the way my friends are looking at me. . . .

"I'm sorry. . . ." I say, and squeak out half a smile. June and Quint exhale. Dirk's fists relax. But as I begin lowering the radio—

I hear it.

The radio is hissing again.

OUR NEXT BROADCAST WILL BE OUR FINAL BROADCAST--
<STATIC>
<CRACKLE>
--WE WILL TRY ONE MORE TIME TONIGHT, AT 10 P.M.--
<STATIC>
<CRACKLE>

Chapter Fourteen

Everyone stares at me. . . .

My arms tremble. I gently set the radio down. I take a shaky step back. I'm scared of the thing.

June's mouth hangs open as she realizes what's happening—then she makes a squeaking sound and races toward the radio.

Quint scratches his head for a moment, then looks up—eyeing the massive rides that tower over us. "Blast . . ." he says. "All this metal and electricity is interfering with the signal. We must reach a higher altitude."

"The Thunder Coaster's big peak is the highest spot in the park," June says. "What about that?"

"A superb suggestion!" Quint exclaims. "The Thunder Coaster! Ingenious, June."

I don't speak. I'm still too stunned. Too overwhelmed.

They begin racing toward the Thunder Coaster. And that's when I hear the horrific sound of skeletal wings beating the air.

The sound snaps me out of my frozen weirdness feeling, and I'm reaching out, grabbing Quint, and shouting, "Guys, take cover!"

I pull Quint, and June and Dirk follow. We dive inside the Fun Land Fried Dough Golden Oil Gazebo, tumbling over a counter, slamming into a mound of stale popcorn. Ants march over the kernels.

An instant later, a shadow sweeps over the ground.

The King Wretch.

The monster soars above the park, circling twice before swooping downward and perching atop the Ferris wheel. The Ferris wheel creaks and bends under the King Wretch's weight.

But the monster doesn't move.

Everyone knows what this means: as long as the King Wretch is there, we're trapped.

We'll miss the radio broadcast. And not just any radio broadcast: the *last* radio broadcast. Everything my friends worked so hard for will be ruined. The thing that is *most* important to them—it's in danger of being lost.

The silence among my friends is deafening.

And the worst part? It's MY fault!

I brought my buddies here! Me! I did that! And the King Wretch is here *because* of me. It's *my head* he filled with weirdo king dreams! It's *my* skull that he stuffed that horrible nightmare inside! It's *me* he wants!

June breaks the silence. "It doesn't look like we're going anywhere," she says with a sigh. "So, you want to talk now, Jack? Or do you want to go back to tantrumming like a little kid?"

I sink into the mound of popcorn. My heart is

racing and sweat is dripping off me, mixing with the cool bite in the air. My stomach is twisted into pretzel knots.

And I'm red-faced.

Not with anger anymore—it actually felt good to let out a full-blown freak-out. Now I'm red with embarrassment—but I swallow that down. Finally, I let it all out. . . .

"Look. I know I've been crazy obsessed with this whole fun thing. It's, like, first you found that radio. We heard those people. And I felt you slipping away. . . . I've been trying so hard to convince you to stay, but . . ."

"But what?" June asks.

"But it was all for nothing."

Quint scoots toward me. "I get it, Jack," he says. "You're afraid that if we get in contact with other people, we might find our families. And you'll be alone."

"But you'll *never* be left alone," June says.

I swallow. I can feel my nose starting to drip and my eyes watering. My lip is even trembling, which is just the most embarrassing—'cause that's always followed by blubbering and blubber snot. "I won't?"

"You won't be alone at all!" June says. "You'll

have your video games and your action figures and your chewed bubble gum collection and your lucky boxers and—"

"Wha—?"

"GOTCHA!" June giggles, then she pounces forward and throws her arms around me. Quint leans over and Dirk comes in, enveloping us all. A long, tight hug—and then we all sink back into our popcorn pit. . . .

I feel tears welling up behind my eyelids. Dirk's right, total wuss stuff. I wipe snot from my nose and grin.

I feel whole. Complete. Recharged. I have *no idea* what's around the corner, but they're right: we'll tackle it together.

"Okay," I say at last. "Enough emotional softy love moment stuff. I can't believe it—but now *I* need to remind *you* about the radio. We have work to do. And we don't have much time."

I stand up, crack my neck 'cause that's a tough guy thing to do, and turn to June and Quint. "I'm getting you to the top of the Thunder Coaster. Tonight. *Now.*"

"But, Jack . . ." June says. "The King Wretch. . . ."

"And it's *me* the King Wretch is after. He's been trying to tell me something. Honestly, he's been, like, *trolling* me. Yeah, that's it—TROLLING!"

Everyone stares at me blankly.

I sigh. "Look, I, ah—I haven't told you guys everything. See, I've encountered the King Wretch twice since the fire station. . . ."

"Come again, friend?" Quint says. "I don't comprehend."

I fidget and swallow. I should have told them this before. I should have told them everything.

"It's simple," I say. "The only way for you guys to use the radio is for me to give him what he wants. He wants a little Jack? Then I'll give him a little Jack. I'm gonna feed the troll.

"Me and that King Wretch, we're going to have a chat. And by have a chat, I mean—well—I probably mean a big epic battle."

Chapter Fifteen

The King Wretch doesn't move from his perch as we race toward the Thunder Coaster. In moments, June, Quint, and I are climbing into the coaster's front car. Dirk turns a crank, and the car is chugalugged up the track. When it finally reaches the peak—a hundred feet above the ground—Dirk locks the crank into place.

I can't help myself. I peek over the side of the car. It's a terrifying, head-spinning view: the car, track, and steps—they all drop off to Fun Land pavement, far, far below. . . .

The track shudders. Dirk's stomping up the steps. June sets the radio down in the car. If we can just keep this radio safe until 10 p.m., we'll be able to hear the final broadcast.

But—

KING WRETCH TAIL WHIP!

I reel back, gasping, heart pounding. The King Wretch is swirling through the air. He looks down, his mouth opens, and he unleashes a blood-chilling *SKREEEE!!!!*

So much for keeping the radio safe . . . his big fat tail just *whomped* it!

No one says anything. I can practically hear their hearts slamming in their chests.

The radio sparks. It's damaged. "How bad?" I ask Quint.

"It is certainly less than good."

"BUT CAN YOU FIX IT?" June asks. Her voice is shaking and bordering on full-out panic. "It's the LAST BROADCAST! At ten! And it's already seven fifteen!"

"We'll get it working," Dirk says. "I promise."

I need to do something, *anything*, to make the King Wretch leave my buddies alone for a while. If I can't, then they won't be able to get the radio working. They'll miss the broadcast.

"You guys fix it," I say. "I'm getting answers. . . ."

'CAUSE NO ONE MESSES WITH MY BUDDIES' ATTEMPTS TO MAKE A RADIO FUNCTION AT A HIGH ALTITUDE!
Worst battle cry ever.
He's not that bright.

I step up onto the roller coaster seat, raising the Louisville Slicer over my head.

"HEY, KING WRETCH!" I scream. "YOU WANT ME?! COME AND GET ME!"

RAAAWRRRRRR!

The King Wretch shrieks and dives. His howl is high-pitched horror—the sound of evil itself. His talons flash open.

"Get the radio out of the car!" I shout. "Quick! Onto the steps, on the side!"

My buddies scramble from the car. Quint sets the radio on the steps, and just in time—

The King Wretch practically takes my head off. His tail whips the car, and there's a sudden squeaking and squealing sound. My stomach turns and my body lurches. The car is going over. . . .

Quint cries, "Jack!" but then I hear nothing except the sound of rusty wheels and screeching metal as the car plummets down the track. The car rattles as it speeds faster along the track.

I grip the coaster bar tight as the wind streams over my face. The momentum propels the car up and over the first dip, then it careens around the next bend and hurtles ahead!

The flying beast snaps out with his talons, tearing into my hoodie and knocking me back. The coaster whips around the next turn, and I'm flung back into the seat. My stomach does an Olympic-type flip. I grip the railing. I'm about to jam the Louisville Slicer into the beast's gut, when—

PLUCK!

One gnarled talon grabs my hoodie. The car plunges down the next drop, but I don't plunge with it—because I'm not inside the car. . . .

This is not going according to plan.

Chapter Sixteen

You think I'm scared right now? WeLL, I'm not! You seem to have me confused with someone who's scared of giant monsters.
FIGHTING GIANT MONSTERS IS BASICALLY MY NUMBER ONE HOBBY!

That's a lie.

I am *very much* scared.

I need to make something clear: I am *not* trained to be an adventurer. I always dreamed of being one, sure. The same way you might dream about playing quarterback for the New

York Giants—even though you are IN NO WAY QUALIFIED TO PLAY QUARTERBACK FOR THE NEW YORK GIANTS.

And in that same vein, I am IN NO WAY QUALIFIED TO HANDLE DANGLING FROM THE TALONS OF A FLYING MONSTER!

Craning my neck, I watch Fun Land shrink away as the King Wretch whisks me through the sky. I get a quick glimpse of my friends atop the Thunder Coaster. They'd better get that radio fixed, or this was all for nothing.

The monster plunges, and I just about swallow my tongue. I look down between my dangling feet. We're, like, sixty feet above the ground.

If I fall? Pancake-splattered-Jack-death action.

And I mean, I love pancakes—chocolate chip with whipped cream, extra butter, mountains of warm maple syrup—but I have zero interest in any *pancake-splattered-Jack-death action*.

We're approaching Comically Speaking. The comic book store is ravaged. Entire walls have collapsed, and it's surrounded by piles of rubble.

And there's something else.

Two parallel lines of monsters stand in front

of the store. I can't quite make out *what* brand of monsters these dudes are, but the stench of evil is extra strong.

I narrow my eyes, trying to figure out what exactly I'm looking at. Just as things are coming into focus, I hear my hoodie tear, the fabric splitting, and then—

I plummet downward for a short moment, and then all I feel is *PAINFUL AWFUL TREE-LIMB-BREAKING-SMASHING ON MY BONES!* And that is my *least favorite bone sensation*!

I crash into a maple tree, then pinball from

branch to branch, wood snapping and cracking. I ricochet into the crook of the tree, and then I'm swinging and splatting to the grass below.

I heave and heave, and at last I scoop up the Louisville Slicer. I shakily get to my feet. It takes a moment for my eyes to focus—but when they do, I realize why we haven't seen any Winged Wretches recently.

They've been here. All of them.

I'm looking at a full horde of Winged Wretches. They stand at attention, like castle guards. But they're staring at me—and I get no sense that they want to attack me or keep me away. What kind of guard doesn't try to keep enemies out?

No, these Winged Wretches are here for a different reason.

They're not guards at all—they're like some sort of nightmarish welcoming committee.

But welcoming me to what?

The King Wretch?

I don't see him. After he dropped me, he disappeared.

But . . . Hmm . . . Yes. *Yes.* I smell him. His odor is permeating the air, seeping through the crumbling walls. And I realize:

He's *inside* Comically Speaking.

I could run. But I won't. And I think the King Wretch knows that.

At this point, I *must* get answers. I *will* do *whatever* it takes to make sure the horrors of the latest vision don't come true.

So I wrap my fingers tight around my blade and I walk forward. . . .

The Winged Wretches do not move. I hear only my sneakers on the snapping autumn leaves. I feel the hot, rancid breath of the Winged Wretches wheezing from their ragged lungs.

I leave the terrifying lineup of monsters behind and push through the door, into Comically Speaking.

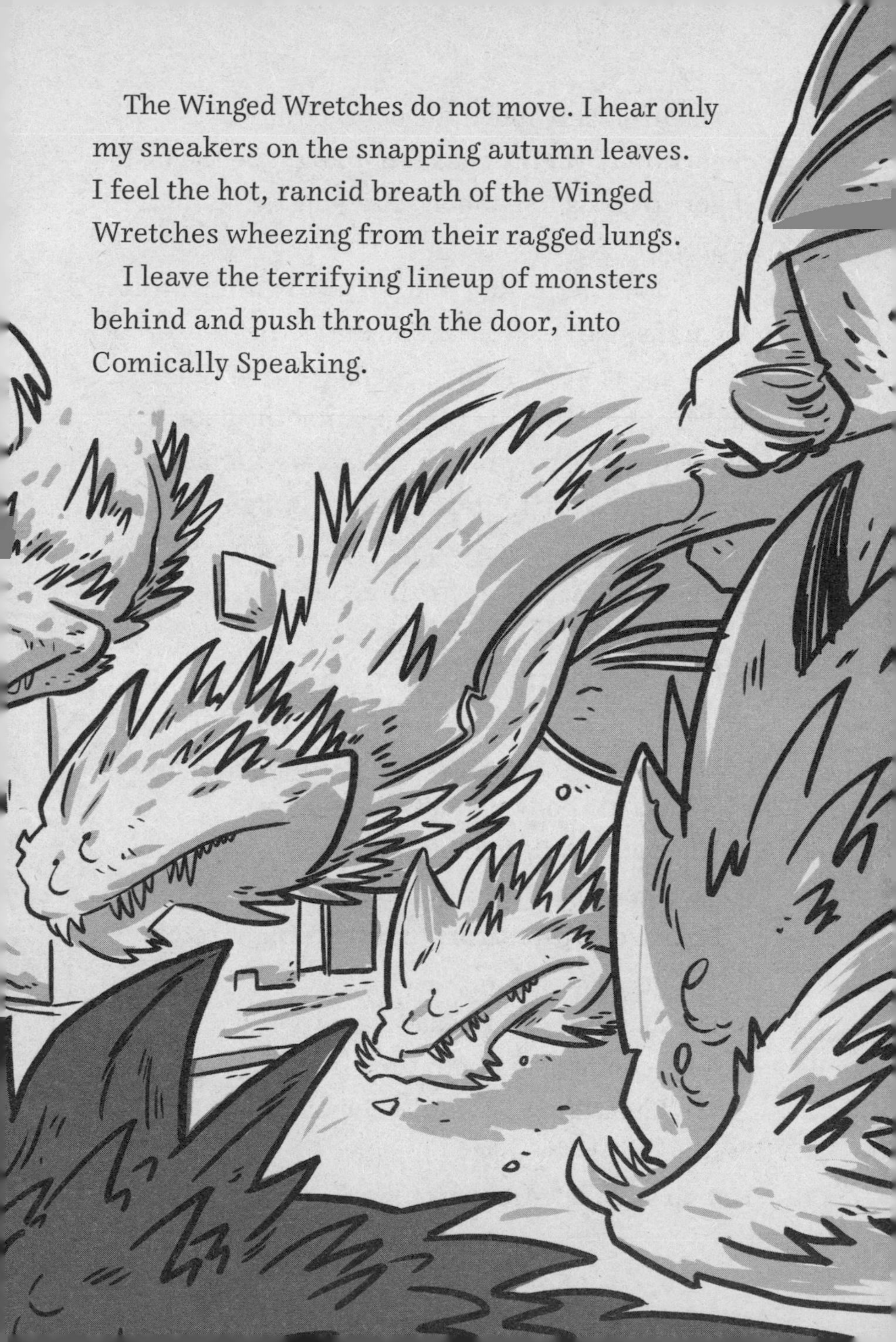

The little bell above the door chimes cheerfully. I get the sense that might be the last cheerful thing to happen for a long while. . . .

SLAM!

The door snaps shut behind me. I gulp, swallow down the fear, and scan the store. The only other exit is blocked. A heap of rubble, action figures, and graphic novels is piled against the door. I spot a few of my favorites. *Calvin and Hobbes*. *Bone*. Heavy stuff, literally—like, weighty, mega-pound books. Curse you, Jeff Smith, for weaving such an extensive, enthralling tale!

The King Wretch is here.

I see his glowing eyes first. And then I see the rest of him: his body is half inside the store, half outside. He lies flat, and the broken wall around him hugs his body and lets in no light.

The rich, foul smell of evil fills the store.

Zombie bones litter the floor.

I realize, with terror, that the King Wretch lives here. . . .

The monster exhales, and a puff of hot air throws comic books into the air.

"Tell me what you want!!" I bark. "What's with the jerky monster lineup outside? And why are you playing games with me? If you want to play games, we can play games—I like lots of games—I like Stratego and I like Minecraft, but I don't like *this*."

The ceiling cracks and splinters as the monster rises, revealing its underbelly. I see a series of armored scales. A spine-chilling sound fills the air—and those scales begin moving and shifting, sliding, revealing something blue and glowing beneath the monster's skin. . . .

And then it happens: the King Wretch's meaty stomach splits open, revealing his insides. But they're not regular gore and guts insides. I'm looking at a strange, fleshy energy window.

And I know exactly what I'm going to see.

Ŗeżżőcħ.

The one who devours worlds.

The one who started this entire Monster Apocalypse.

The one who nearly came through into our world.

The one I stopped once before.

The King Wretch's head rolls back in pain, and from the depths of his being comes a deafening roar that shakes my soul. The blue underbelly flashes and flickers. It reminds me of the old TV at the first orphanage I stayed at—you had to fiddle with the antenna to get the reception just right.

Last time around, Ŗeżżőcħ spoke through a strange, magical tree. Now it is the belly of a beast—literally.

The King Wretch's howls increase and their pitch changes and the reception adjusts—and then I'm staring at Ŗeżżőcħ. And for the first time, Ŗeżżőcħ speaks to me. . . .

JACK SULLIVAN. IT IS A PLEASURE TO MEET YOU, FINALLY. DO YOU KNOW WHO I AM?
Ŗeżżőcȟ the Ancient, Destructor of Worlds.

"I saw you," I say. "When Thrull tried to bring you into this world. To devour it."

Ŗeżżőcȟ's voice is an awful whisper. "AND I SAW YOU. I WAS *IMPRESSED* BY YOU. YOU ARE A BRAVE BOY. A STRONG BOY."

"Strong? You think? I mean, I never did any bench-pressing or anything, but—"

"STRONG WHERE IT MATTERS," Ŗeżżőcȟ interrupts. "INSIDE. YOUR INNER SELF IS MIGHTY."

I flinch, and I blink about a dozen times. Am I really being complimented by a powerful war demon and destructor from another universe? I mean, that was never a Feat of

Apocalyptic Success, but it should be. I'll take the compliment!

Ŗeżżőcħ says, "I BELIEVE WE GOT OFF ON THE WRONG FOOT, AS IT WERE. I AM A FAN OF YOURS."

"Oh really?" I snap. "Then why have you been hunting me with your—your—King Wretch here?"

"THE ŜŖŒČĘĦ? THE CREATURE YOU REFER TO AS THE KING WRETCH? I ONLY WISHED TO SPEAK WITH YOU. THAT IS WHY THE MONSTER SAVED YOU FROM THE UNDEAD. I SIMPLY WANTED YOUR ATTENTION, JACK."

"My attention?" I ask, not understanding or believing. "And Rover? My pet monster? My friend? You *hurt* him."

"AS I SAID, YOUR ATTENTION WAS NEEDED. SO, YES, I HURT HIM. WHAT IS ONE MONSTER, JACK, WHEN WE ARE DISCUSSING THE FUTURE OF YOUR WORLD?"

"Hurting my monster-dog is *not* the way to get on my good side."

"ENOUGH!" Ŗeżżőcħ barks. "I NEEDED TO SHOW YOU YOUR CHOICES."

"Those strange dream-vision-thingies?"

"IF THAT IS THE TERM YOU USE, THEN YES. TELL ME: WHAT DID YOU SEE IN THE FIRST?"

I hesitate. I can't be talking to this monster. I can't. But I feel unable to move. Not frozen, like before—just *overwhelmed*.

Ŗeżżőcħ says, "YOU WERE STRONG IN THE FIRST VISION, JACK. YOU WERE A KING. YOU WOULD HAVE SAT BY MY SIDE. AND YOUR FRIENDS. HOW WERE THEY?"

"They were okay," I say. I shrug nervously. "I guess."

"THEY ARE VERY IMPORTANT TO YOU, AREN'T THEY? I SAW YOU WITH THEM, FROM THE TREE OF ENTRY."

"Yes, they're important," I say.

"AND THE SECOND CHOICE I SHOWED YOU? WHAT DID YOU SEE?"

"It was a nightmare."

"HOW WERE YOUR FRIENDS THEN?"

I don't respond.

"YOU WERE ALONE," Ŗeżżőcħ says. He speaks slower now. Every word is steady and hard. "EVERYTHING YOU LOVED: GONE. YOUR HOME BURNED. YOU HAD NOTHING. YOU WOULD NEVER HAVE ANYTHING AGAIN. I WILL COME INTO THIS WORLD, JACK. I WILL. BUT I DO NOT WISH TO DEVOUR IT, AS YOU SUSPECTED."

"You . . . you don't?" I ask.

"ON THE CONTRARY, I WOULD LIKE YOUR WORLD TO THRIVE. I NEED A NEW HOME. A PERMANENT HOME. THE ONLY QUESTION IS—WHEN I COME INTO THIS WORLD, HOW WILL I BE WELCOMED? YOU CAN DECIDE," he says. "WILL IT BE THE DREAM? OR WILL IT BE THE NIGHTMARE? THAT IS UP TO YOU."

I shake my head, like my brain is an Etch A Sketch I can wipe clean. I don't want this responsibility. I don't want to fight this villain. I want to stop him, sure—but really, I just want to go back to the tree house and barbecue and play video games with my buddies.

Ŗeżżőcħ suddenly roars, "DO YOU REALIZE YOUR IMPORTANCE? YOU PLAY A VITAL ROLE IN THE FUTURE OF THIS WORLD YOU CALL HOME. THRULL WAS FORMIDABLE, BUT HE WAS UNABLE TO COMPLETE THE TASK I GAVE HIM. I NEED SOMEONE OF THIS WORLD. AND HUMANS APPEAR TO BE THE ONLY INTELLIGENT BEINGS IN THIS DIMENSION."

"Hey!" I bark. "You ever meet a golden retriever? They are SHARP. Cats, ehh, take 'em or leave 'em. But don't badmouth puppies!"

"BOY, YOU ARE EASILY DISTRACTED," Ŗeżżőcħ says. "DO NOT BE. COME HERE. . . ."

I don't want to, but I step closer.

The King Wretch's head lowers and his eyes swirl and it begins—one final dream-vision-thingy—one final nightmare. . . .

I stand alone.

I'm not sure where.

I'm in a city I don't recognize.

I see my friends reunited with their families. June hugs her parents. Quint's mom scoops him up and his dad cries happy tears. Even Dirk—he's hugging a sister I didn't know existed.

And then I see me.

Wandering like some sort of wasteland warrior. Which is pretty cool, I guess, but I'm alone. Mostly.

I have Rover.

No Quint. No June. No Dirk. No Bardle. No Biggun. No Skaelka. No family. Just a boy and his monster-dog.

And I feel the emotion of that.

I'm not just *seeing* it. It's not just a dream or a vision. I'm feeling that pain—the brutal agony of being alone.

It's a choking feeling. Like a hand twisting my heart, pulling at the parts of me that are most vulnerable.

And then . . .

And then I come tumbling out of the nightmarish vision. I'm facing Ŗeżżőcħ again. And he's beckoning me. Calling to me. Asking for my help . . .

HELP ME, JACK. BRING ME INTO THIS WORLD, AND YOU NEED NOT LOSE ANYONE AGAIN. YOU CAN BE A KING.

BUT IF YOU CHOOSE NOT TO HELP ME, YOU WILL LOSE EVERYTHING. YOUR FRIENDS WILL LEAVE YOU. AND WHEN I DO COME—I WILL DESTROY THEM AS WELL. . . .

Chapter Seventeen

Heroes surround me. The comic book store is full of them.

I'm circled by life-size cardboard cutouts from movies and comics, and I feel like they're watching me. Luke Cage. Gambit. Obi-Wan Kenobi. Wonder Woman. Ash Ketchum.

Growing up an orphan, I was raised by these heroes, in a way. They showed me how to act, how to *be*.

Could I be tempted by Ŗeżżőcħ? I don't know. Maybe. I'm not perfect.

But to *fold*? To *give in*?

To *abandon* all good in hopes of saving my own skin? In front of these guys?

As Wolverine would say: "No way, bub."

If Ŗeżżőcħ wanted my help, Comically Speaking was the wrong place to bargain. . . .

The ground rocks as the King Wretch's talons pierce and split the floor. In the fleshy window, Ŗeżżőcħ growls. "SO BE IT, *HERO*. IF YOU WILL NOT HELP ME, YOU WILL BE ELIMINATED. I WILL FIND *ANOTHER* HUMAN TO USHER ME INTO EARTH."

The King Wretch's head jerks upward and I see pain rack his body. His tail slithers, snakes, and snaps as Ŗeżżőcħ growls, "NOW, JACK SULLIVAN, I WILL WATCH AS YOU PERISH, ALONE. . . ."

A voice suddenly slices through the room: *"He won't be alone anytime soon!"*

I whirl around. June! The rear door's barricade is being tossed to the side. I see Biggun clearing the rubble and my friends rushing inside. Dirk stomps, carrying the High-Strike hammer, and—

The King Wretch howls and buckles!

Ŗeżżőcħ flashes and emits a pained cry. I know he's not *hurt* hurt, but we have snapped him out of his portal—and now his voice is slithering, thinning.

Ŗeżżőcħ gives a single, final order to the King Wretch: "TAKE YOUR FOLLOWERS AND DESTROY THE TOWN! DESTROY THE MONSTERS THAT LIVE THERE! DESTROY JACK'S FRIENDS! LEAVE YOUNG JACK FOR LAST. . . . I WANT HIM TO SEE THE MISTAKE HE HAS MADE. . . . I WANT TO SEE HIM SUFFER. . . ."

The King Wretch snarls, and then with a tremendous burst, the monster erupts upward and rockets through the ceiling, and vanishes.

I turn to my friends. We need to hurry—but I just want to spend a second taking them in.

"Did you see that freaking *army* of Winged Wretches outside?" I ask.

"Yep," Dirk says. "Why do you think we took the back door?"

"They're still out there . . ." I say, trying to wrap my head around that horror—but then I think of something else entirely: "Wait! *THE RADIO!* What happened with the radio?"

"It's still on the roller coaster," June says.

"Wait—but—you left it?" I ask. "It's alone there, unprotected?!"

June simply says, "We were in a hurry to save our friend."

I don't know how to respond. The radio was so important. The radio was EVERYTHING. And now it's just sitting there, unprotected, at the top of the Thunder Coaster. But—

WHAP! WHAP! WHAP!

We all whirl. A new sound: like an army of helicopters lifting off in some awesome Arnold action movie.

I push open the front door. The tiny bell chimes again—a reminder that we're in a small-town comic book store. We're someplace *normal* and *wholesome* and *okay*. And that makes it all worse, because what I'm looking at is so *not normal* and *not wholesome* and *not okay*.

All twelve Winged Wretches are rising, following their leader, the King Wretch.

Ŗeżżőcħ ordered the King Wretch to destroy the town—and that's what he's doing. The King Wretch is taking his army to make that second, horrific nightmare-vision—tree house burning, friends gone, monsters destroyed—become a cold and gruesome reality. . . .

"C'mon, gang. We've got friends to save, evil to defeat, and butt-whoopin' to do."

Chapter Eighteen

RUINATION À LA REZZOCH!

When we reach the Town Square, it's chaos. The battle unfolds in the streets, on the rooftops, on the ground, and in the air.

The Winged Wretches attack while the

King Wretch circles high above, watching his minions.

If this was, like, *Star Trek*, the King Wretch would be like the mother ship and these Winged Wretches would be his sentinels of badness.

Bardle greets us with sword in hand. "Jack!" he growls. "I smell evil on these beasts."

I nod. "The King Wretch is a servant of Ŗeżżőcħ. These are his soldiers."

"Ŗeżżőcħ . . ." Bardle snarls. "Then we must—"

Before he can finish his sentence, a flash of movement cuts through the darkness. And then Bardle is gone! Plucked from the ground by a Winged Wretch!

"Bardle!" Quint cries out.

The Winged Wretch circles, its talons snap open, and Bardle is dropped onto the Town Green. The ground shakes. I watch the Ridionculous Radical Triumph Trophy topple from its place atop the statue and crash to the grass beside him.

The trophy. The *games*.

I wonder . . .

And as I wonder, another Winged Wretch scoops up the monster Gwif and *hurls* her into Joe's Pizza. The building nearly crumbles.

I've seen this before, in the vision. This is how it begins. And I know how it ends, too. With everyone inside Joe's Pizza: *destroyed*.

Everything we've built replaced by devastation.

I *cannot* let it come true.

What if there was another way? Not the first vision, where I do what Ŗeżżőcħ tells me and I'm rewarded with kingly respect and a kick-butt throne. But not the second vision, either, where I disobey and my punishment destroys everyone I care about.

What if I could come up with my *own* vision for the future, something the King Wretch never showed me?

Maybe the solution is in the trophy and what it represents. Monsters and humans, being awesome, side by side. . . .

Everyone! Fight like these are THE MONSTERS VERSUS HUMANS ALMIGHTY ULTRA-IMPORTANT TOURNAMENT GAMES!
Play to win! Together!

Amid the chaos and combat, I catch the eyes of a few monsters. Are they *really* about to take orders from a nasally voiced little kid with a Little League bat?

Skaelka raises her ax high and roars. "You heard the boy! Do as he says! We shall decapitate this big beast!"

Bardle is rising, using his sword to stand. "Jack and his friends stopped Ŗeżżőcħ once before!" he shouts. "Together, we will do it again!"

I take a deep breath, look to the sky, and holler, "TOURNAMENT GAME: *DODGEBALL!*"

At once, everything that isn't tied *down* is thrown *up*. Splintered park benches hurled at the winged beasts. Lamp posts fly like javelins! I watch a trash barrel explode against the side of a Winged Wretch. The monsters howl in pain.

"TOURNAMENT GAME: KICKBALL!" I bark. The park's water fountain is drop-kicked into the face of a diving Winged Wretch. It explodes in a blast of stone and piping.

I whirl around as I hear a voice call out, "I prefer chopping!"

It's Skaelka—she's leaping from the roof of Simard's Roast Beef and *chopping* at a Winged

Wretch. She lands atop the beast, grips the monster's hide, and brings her ax crashing down in a heavy chop. The Winged Wretch howls, corkscrews through the air, then plummets into the street in an eruption of pavement.

Skaelka hops off, grinning. "Not decapitated!" she barks. "But a start!"

"TOURNAMENT GAME: HUMAN TOSSING!" one monster yells.

Wait up. Hold on. Did that monster just say, "Human tossing"? Huh? No. NO!

"I meant the other games!" I cry out. "Not human tossing! No tossing of humans!"

But it's too late. Biggun has scooped up Quint. My buddy is a bony little human missile about to be fired into the sky. I cry out, "DON'T!" and manage to throw myself onto Biggun's arm just as he hurls Quint. Quint flips through the air and flops onto the Town Green.

"Sorry, Biggun!" I squeak out. "Quint's not made for tossing! He's delicate!"

As I hurry to Quint, I spot a metallic glimmer: the Ridonculous Radical Triumph Trophy. The shiny glint of the razor-sharp tip gives me an idea. . . .

"Dirk!" I shout. "The trophy! Muscles, please!"

In an instant, Dirk is there, lifting it. Skaelka appears, helping to hoist the trophy high.

"To the tree house!" I shout. "If we can knock the King Wretch out of commission, then his army of Winged Wretches will leave us alone! Maybe? Hopefully? I mean—that's how video game boss fights work!"

RAWWWWWRRR!

The King Wretch's spine-chilling roar pierces the night air—and every single Winged Wretch instantly dives toward us.

"GRRR-UNT."

It's Biggun. He's looking down at me. I think I even detect a slight nod, like he's saying, "I got this, homeslice. Go."

June calls out, "JACK! I'll stay with Biggun and buy you some time. NOW GET MOVING, DUDE!"

So we run. And behind us, Biggun and June go to work—fists flying, spear slashing, and Wretches getting wrecked. . . .

Dirk and Skaelka lug the trophy to the tree house. We all scale the ladder to the top level, where our most fearsome tree house weapon awaits.

"Jam the trophy into the Colossal Crossbow!" I say, and Skaelka does.

"Together!" Dirk says, and at once, we're tugging on the heavy drawstring and sliding the trophy into place. "We must get the monster's attention!" Quint says. He takes charge, wrapping his finger around the crossbow's trigger.

"On it!" I shout, hopping down a level and grabbing hold of the BallBlaster 2000. I pretend the King Wretch is Conan the Barbarian and—*PWAP! PWAP! PWAP!* A stream of tennis balls pounds the King Wretch's hide.

"Hey, King Wretch! Here I am!" I scream. "Didn't you just *hate* when I totally defied you in the comic book store? Well, here I am! Come get me!"

In a flash,the great beast is slicing toward the tree house. And Quint is still aiming . . .

"Not yet . . ." Quint says. He patiently stares down the length of the bow.

"Dude, the King Wretch is right there!" I bark as I climb back up. I see Quint's finger on the crossbow trigger—and I'm thinking about how he's always choking under pressure. I mean, he's Quint the Choker!

But I *must* have faith in my buddy now, because that's what buddies are for: having faith in!

"Not yet," Quint repeats.

The King Wretch's mouth opens wide, ferocious fangs flashing. "NOW!" Quint cries as he pulls the trigger and—

“BOOM! YES! Right down the ol’ piehole!” I exclaim. “Nice shooting, Quint!”

Quint whirls, smiling wide. “In your FACE, friend! I am SPLENDID under pressure! What do I always tell you, Jack? It’s all about being dexterous, and I am *quite* dexterous!”

I shrug, then flash him a teasing grin. “Maybe, but you still can’t fly a Helidrone for squat.”

“DOWN!” Dirk yells, and just in time. . . .

The roof of the tree house erupts in a furious blast of wood and bark and movie posters as the King Wretch explodes through.

I lift my head. Action figures spill off me. I flick them away and watch the King Wretch spiral through the air, hacking and coughing.

We hurt him.

Bad.

Just then, I see Dirk yanking a coil of rope from his backpack. He leaps from the tree house to the ground below.

“What’s he playing at?” Quint asks.

Dirk is whirling the rope over his head. He cries out, “Cowboy Dirk, reporting for duty!” and then . . .

"We need to get the King Wretch away from the town," I say. "Or there won't *be* a town."

But where do we lead this blasted beast?

I stand, thinking, and brushing bits of demolished tree house off me. Looking down I see scraps of wood. *Junk*.

And I know *just* what to do.

"Listen up, monster buds and humans!" I shout. "FINAL TOURNAMENT GAME is a new one. LASSO! Rope this beast!"

The King Wretch jerks and spasms. His flying is jagged and uneven.

I'm scooping up a coil of rope when I hear one tremendously gnarly sound. . . .

BLUHHYYHHEARCKKKKK!

Vomit. An eruption of blue-red puke splatters the ground, and the trophy follows.

The King Wretch is no longer choking.

Now he's just extra, extra mad.

"LASSOS!" I shout, and at once, they fly, coming from every angle.

They loop around the King Wretch's legs and bring the beast to a jarring midair halt! The monster thrashes and furiously beats his wings.

The smaller Winged Wretches fly upward and then circle slowly. They seem confused by their king's sudden helplessness.

"We're gonna run this monster straight out of town!" I shout. "C'mon, Rover!"

But wait . . . Where *is* Rover? Is he, like, sitting this fight out? On the sidelines? That doesn't sound like my monster-dog.

But then I hear him, growling and woofing.

Bardle is at the door to Joe's Pizza. He flashes a smile, opens the door, and Rover charges out.

I gasp.

Bardle and Dirk's Rover-protection project is complete. And, man, oh man, it is *righteous*.

They have *armored* my buddy Rover!

I wasn't far off—it *is* like a video game, and Rover *has* leveled up! It's like, y'know: *Rover, Scrap Armor, UNLOCKED. LEVEL 2*.

Rover looks to the sky. His eyes burn with anger as he watches the King Wretch. His mouth is drawn back and his jagged teeth drip saliva. He wants—let's be honest—*revenge*.

And I'm happy to help.

Chapter Nineteen

Buildings seem to race past. The street is a blur beneath us.

See, we might have the King Wretch lassoed, but *he's* pulling us—and I'm hanging on for dear life. Rover's feet charge, keeping up—if he slows down, I'll be *yanked* from the saddle.

But one tiny bit of relief: the Winged Wretches are not following. They continue swirling above the Town Square like buzzards.

"This is not fantastic, Jack!" Quint shouts, as he *whips* past me, dragged by the King Wretch. "The King Wretch is too large! We need *our own* oversized monster if we have any hope of defeating him!"

"We have one!" I say. "And that's where I'm trying to go!"

We race farther, faster, Rover's feet pounding the ground. The King Wretch thrashes, jerking the BoomKarts and Big Mama back and forth across the street. Only Biggun's tremendous strength keeps us from being simply plucked into the sky.

We need to lead this parade.

"Let him have it!" I holler. "Fire! Unload! Blitz the beast with everything we've got!"

KRAKA-BOOMKART!
KRAKA-BIGGUN!

The pounding slows the King Wretch. I pull Rover's reins tighter as we race around the next corner. But then . . .

WHOOSH!

The King Wretch's wings snap, he soars upward, and—

YANK!

Every lasso is *ripped* from our hands! My palms sting with ultimate rope burn. The King Wretch is free. . . .

Glancing back, I see Big Mama and the BoomKarts skid to a stop at the side of the road. They can no longer keep up. Quint and June and Skaelka and Bardle and Biggun and Dirk can only watch.

It's just me, Rover, and the King Wretch now. . . .

The King Wretch loops back around, knifing through the air. The lassos dangle from his leg.

I hold Rover tight, my senses suddenly hyperpeaked. I smell the nearby scrapyard. . . .

Rover lowers his head.

I lean forward, crouched over him.

"Rover, buddy," I whisper. "Let's do this."

Beneath me, Rover stampedes faster and faster. I feel his ribs quake. He growls, an angry sound from the depths of his belly. And then—

I want to shut my eyes, but I don't.

The King Wretch is screaming toward us. His wings are tremendously dark things, leathery and bony. His eyes are alight with a terrible green fury. The monster's mouth opens to devour us.

I see fangs, flashing.

I see goo, dripping.

I see darkness, waiting.

But I don't pull back. I lean forward.

Rover bears down, speeding toward the enemy. And then—

I tug on the reins!

My seat jerks. My arm's buck. And at the last possible second—

Rover *leaps*! There's a deafening—

SLAKKKK!!!!

The King Wretch's talons *slam* into Rover's head. They rake his side and clip my shoulder, but I hang on tight. Rover's armor holds.

I owe my man Bardle a milk shake—he just saved my monster-dog from being smashed, gashed, and brain-bashed.

And when Rover lands, all six lassos are clenched tight in his teeth.

Run, Rover! Straight ahead! It's me to take out the trash . . .
Or, actuaLLy, maybe it's time to bring in the trash? Deliver the junk?
Whatever— LET'S DO THIS!

Rover races. The King Wretch is jerked through the air. He screeches and howls and beats his wings, trying to take off—trying to escape. But he's like a kite twirling about in a tornado—a tornado with Rover strength. . . .

Big Al's Junk Palace looms up ahead. I see the trash mountain moving. Perhaps the Scrapken senses the battle going on right outside his lair.

Stampeding, riding, fast, hard, closing in, and then—

"ROVER!" I shout from the depths of my lungs. "BRAKES! NOW!"

Rover's nails puncture the pavement. He stops so short I'm nearly flung over the front. The momentum snaps the King Wretch forward, into Big Al's Junk Palace. . . .

CRASH!

It seems to happen in slow motion.

The King Wretch is chopped through the air.

And as I watch the enemy being whipped downward, I think—for an instant—I see the face of Ŗeżżőcħ again. I see it in the strange, horrific underbelly of the King Wretch.

Ŗeżżőcħ is watching me. Not done with me.

But I'm done with him.

I narrow my eyes, and as the King Wretch is about to slam into the scrapyard—

I swing my blade and the Louisville Slicer cuts clean through the lassos. The monster is released. Junk and metal explodes, deafeningly loud, as the King Wretch smashes into the scrap heap.

Calm for a second.

Quiet.

And then, junk erupting, the Scrapken appearing, wrapping its tremendous tentacles around the King Wretch. . . .

CLASH OF THE BIG BAD MONSTERS!

Howls.

Shrieks.

Roars.

Slithery serpent sounds and then, at last, the King Wretch goes silent. The Scrapken hugs him anaconda tight, squeezing, crushing, and then they disappear beneath the scrap, into the ground. . . .

Chapter Twenty

My chest heaves. I'm flat on Rover's back, catching my breath. I scratch behind his ears. And I just lie there, feeling my armored battle buddy pant and puff.

When I finally sit up, I see my friends.

Every human, every monster. They're all grinning.

They saved us. We saved them. That's how it should be.

I look beyond my friends, to the Town Square in the distance. The Winged Wretches are scattering. Now that they no longer have their king to answer to, they simply swirl off into the night. . . .

"Wait! What time is it?" June suddenly asks.

Quint looks to the sky. "Based on the position of the Big Dipper and the North Star, I'd guess it is—and this is an approximate guess—8:17. But don't hold me to that! It could be 8:19 or even 8:20. I cannot say with complete precision."

"We still have time!" June exclaims. "The final broadcast is at ten p.m.!"

A massive smile appears on my face as I look to the crowd. "Hey, monsters—you ever been to this thing called an amusement park?"

And soon . . .

Dirk pushes up another Thunder Coaster car. We huddle together inside it, high atop the Thunder Coaster. Beside us, on the steps, Rover is curled into a ball. Quint finishes repairing the radio and we wait.

I watch the monsters having a blast: playing games, enjoying the rides. And then, I can't help it—I'm too happy, too proud—and I stand up and I exclaim—

Instantly, I plop back down, totally red-faced. But there's no need to be embarrassed. June throws her arm around me and pulls me tight, shoulder to shoulder, and Dirk and I bump fists and Quint just beams.

"It's almost time," Quint says.

And then the big clock at the center of the park strikes ten times.

We all lean forward, eyes on the radio, breath held.

But nothing happens.

Just . . . nothing.

We wait five minutes.

Ten minutes.

Thirty minutes.

In the moonlight, I can see June gulp back her grief. Her shoulder twitches and she wipes at her eyes. And just then, it begins to spit rain. It's not a hard rain, but it's cold and icy. We huddle tighter.

Quint holds out a hand, and rain splashes against his palm. "This will be our first winter during the Monster Apocalypse," he says quietly.

"Should we wait longer?" Dirk asks.

June shrugs. "There's no point, I guess."

Quint begins packing up the radio. "Don't worry, June. We'll have it with us. You never know when someone might come on."

"But the reception is best here. . . ." June says softly. The gloom I hear in her voice is visible on her face.

"You know what?" I say. "We just crushed some serious evil. We saved Earth—*again*. I'm not afraid of a little rain or a little height. I'm sleeping up here. Tonight. With the radio. Maybe whoever's on the other end just got held up or something. Maybe they're on the toilet or they got, like, really into some movie they're watching and they forgot to call! We'll wait."

June looks up, eyes wide and wet. "Really?"

I nod. "Really."

Dirk and I retrieve a bunch of Fun Land sweatshirts from a shop, and we turn them into blankets. I curl up.

June is sitting up straight, staring at the radio. She's the last thing I see as I drift off to sleep.

It's nearly dawn when the radio crackles. I look to rouse June, but there's no need—she's awake. It doesn't look like she's moved an inch all night. Quint and Dirk hear the radio, too, and rise. Even Rover lifts his head.

I look to my friends.

No one speaks. Not even June.

The rain is falling heavier now, and I huddle tight under my sweatshirts. I blow onto my hands to warm them. And then, with a happy shrug, I say, “Well? Whaddya guys wanna do now?”

THE END! (for now . . .)

But do not worry!

Jack, Quint, June, Dirk, and Rover will return!

Acknowledgments

THE BIGGEST THANKS to Douglas Holgate, for being the best drawer of giant monsters in the history of giant monster drawers. Leila Sales, my brilliant and insightful editor—I can't say thank you enough. Jim Hoover for going above and beyond, time after time. Bridget Hartzler and everyone else in Viking's wonderful publicity and marketing department—thank you for all that you do! And of course, Ken Wright—thank you for believing and supporting this series.

Dan Lazar, my agent at Writers House, for everything. Cecilia de la Campa and James Munro, for helping the Last Kids travel the world. Torie Doherty-Munro, for dealing with me, 'cause I'm definitely annoying. Kassie Evashevski at UTA for working so hard to take this to the next level.

My oldest and bestest friends, who send me long, long, long group texts full of ideas: Chris Amaru, Geoff Baker, Mike Mandolese, Matt McArdle, Forever and Always Mike Ryan (you dope), Marty Strandberg, Ben Murphy.

My parents. Obviously.

And Alyse. My perfect wife. I love you. And I love you for bringing wonderful Lila into the world.

To be very clear: this book is not for Ruby.

© Ruby Brallier

MAX BRALLIER!

is the *New York Times* bestselling author of more than thirty books and games, including the Last Kids on Earth series. He writes both children's books and adult books, including the Galactic Hot Dogs series and the pick-your-own-path adventure *Can YOU Survive the Zombie Apocalypse?* He has written books for properties including *Adventure Time, Regular Show, Steven Universe, Uncle Grandpa,* and *Poptropica.*

Under the pen name Jack Chabert, he is the creator and author of the Eerie Elementary series for Scholastic Books as well as the author of the *New York Times* bestelling graphic novel *Poptropica: Book 1: Mystery of the Map.* Previously, he worked in the marketing department at St. Martin's Press. Max lives in New York with his wife, Alyse, who is way too good for him. His daughter, Lila, is simply the best.

The author building his own tree house as a kiddo.

DOUGLAS HOLGATE!

has been a freelance comic book artist and illustrator based in Melbourne, Australia, for more than ten years. He's illustrated books for publishers such as HarperCollins, Penguin Random House, Hachette, and Simon & Schuster, including the Planet Tad series, *Cheesie Mack*, *Case File 13*, and *Zoo Sleepover*.

Douglas has illustrated comics for Image, Dynamite, Abrams, and Penguin Random House. He's currently working on the self-published series Maralinga, which received grant funding from the Australian Society of Authors and the Victorian Council for the Arts, as well as the all-ages graphic novel *Clem Hetherington and the Ironwood Race*, published by Scholastic Graphix, both co-created with writer Jen Breach.